A two-handed game

Catherine knew all too well the rules of the game of let's-pretend-to-be-in-love she was hired to play by the Duke of Clarendon. She had no claim on his affections, just as he had none on hers.

Thus, when Clarendon renewed his intimacy with the beautiful and notorious Lady Blanche Romney, Catherine had no excuse for anger.

And when Catherine encouraged the ardent admiration of such clearly smitten gentlemen as the handsome Lord Charles Musgrave and the wickedly worldly Marquess of Lynsford, the duke had no reason for rage.

Love free from fetters was most certainly a game that two could play.

And both could lose. . . .

The
False Fiancée

Emma Lange

A SIGNET BOOK

NEW AMERICAN LIBRARY

Copyright © 1987 by Emma Lange

SIGNET, SIGNET CLASSIC, MENTOR, ONYX, PLUME,
MERIDIAN and NAL BOOKS are published by NAL PENGUIN INC.,
1633 Broadway, New York, New York 10019

First Printing, May, 1987

1 2 3 4 5 6 7 8 9

PRINTED IN THE UNITED STATES OF AMERICA

1

"*I* will not tolerate such indignity. No! And no! I insist you put that scheming little doxy in her place."

Madame Rosa Cassello, leading lady at the Theatre Royal, in Bath, was a large woman with a voice to match. Capable of projecting even a whisper to the farthest reaches of the theater, Mme Rosa was capable of roaring when, as on this occasion, she was angry.

"Now, Rosa, calm yourself, please. It is good for business when the young bucks appreciate all of our players."

Mr. Adolphus Trevinian, the manager of the theater, had, in marked contrast to his principal actress, a soothing voice. Although Mr. Trevinian's voice could not be heard throughout the theater, it could be heard very easily in the cramped dressing room adjoining Mme Rosa's.

In this room the four supporting actresses who had roles in the theater's current production were changing from their stage costumes into their after-theater dresses. Three of the four women were quite obviously listening to the exchange occurring next door, stopping frequently to roll their eyes over a particularly outrageous remark or to titter at one of Mr. Trevinian's conciliatory replies. Occasionally they would cast quick, speculative glances toward the fourth member of their group. Unlike the others, she did

not seem to be listening to the exchange in the next
room, but seemed instead to be concentrating exclu-
sively on the simple task of wiping her face free of
greasepaint.

"It may be good for your business to encourage
that creature, but it is unbearable that I"—here Mme
Rosa's voice rose to a new crescendo—"Mme Rosa
Cassello should have my lines interrupted by applause for her—a bag of bones who has not been an
actress for even a year."

One of the younger actresses in the adjoining room
clapped her hand over her mouth to stifle the laughter threatening to spill out. All three actresses again
turned toward the young woman who had now succeeded in removing all of the paint from her face.
Despite the charged atmosphere in the little room,
she remained aloof, with a closed expression on her
delicate, young face. Only the tight line of her full
lips indicated that she, too, was fully aware of the
altercation taking place in the adjoining room. Standing, she walked to a long rack and selected from
among the various costumes hanging upon it a drab
gray woolen dress and a heavy brown pelisse.

Her choice of dress was remarkable only in contrast to that of the other actresses. For, while the
wool dress and heavy pelisse would serve to protect
her from the cold March winds buffeting Bath, they
were not nearly as fine, nor as revealing, as the shiny
taffetas with plunging necklines that her confeder-
ates had chosen.

"Do something about her, Adolph, or I shall leave
this shabby excuse for a theater. I have been offered
a position in Glasgow, I warn you."

Two of the young actresses pretended to applaud
this threat, but the plainly dressed young woman
fixed her attention on pushing every wisp of her
long, lustrous auburn hair under an old, dingy bonnet. With a last glance in the mirror above her dress-

ing table, she adjusted the brim of her bonnet to shade her eyes. Apparently satisfied, the young woman left the dressing room without a backward glance, not pausing until she reached a door at the back of the theater.

As she approached, the door suddenly swung open, presenting to her view a long line of fashionable young Tulips all shouting while they jumped up to get a better view. Cursing angrily, an older man who had been standing before the door wrested it from the first young buck and slammed it shut.

"Damned no-good rotters! They'll be the death of me," he grumbled to himself.

"You're a brave man, Mr. Phillips."

Phillips jerked around at the sound of the clear, well-spoken voice behind him. The young woman's head was tilted back so that he could see a pair of remarkable amber eyes, framed by dark, thick lashes, sparkling at him.

For a moment, Phillips, an actor well past his prime whose principal responsibility was to guard the theater's back entrance, was lost in admiration of those eyes. A light-amber flecked with gold, they often changed color as they reflected the young actress's mood. Tonight, lightened with laughter, they reminded him of jewels—topazes perhaps—flashing in the sun. Aye, she's a real beauty, Phillips thought to himself, and not stuck on herself neither, he added, taking in the glowing smile on her face.

"They're all clamorin' for ye tonight, Miss Wright. You be cautious and don't let 'em see who's under that mountain o' clothes ye got on."

"I shall watch my step, Mr. Phillips." The young actress's smile widened. "I do believe I save my best acting for my performance as an old hag."

A door banged behind them and the voice of Mme Rosa could be heard again, though more faintly.

The young woman's smile faded and her jaw tightened. "I believe that is my cue to go, Mr. Phillips. I am far too tired to listen to any more of her harangues now."

"She's just jealous of ye, Miss Wright, and that's a fact."

"Whatever the cause, Mr. Phillips, I am afraid the result of her anger will be to have me fired." Miss Wright's lovely eyes seemed to dim at the prospect. Then, raising her chin with a touch of defiance, she added lightly, "But enough of this, I must get on my way. Open the portals, please, Mr. Phillips."

Phillips opened the door and before his eyes the willowy, young beauty of slightly more than medium height, standing erect in heavy, ill-fitting clothes, was transformed into a bent, stiff crone on whom the tired, old garments looked completely natural.

The hag scuttled down the narrow alley, quite free from the scrutiny of the young bucks who ignored such an ugly thing and used the opportunity presented by the opened door to attempt to push past Phillips. The old man kept their attention on the door until the crone had disappeared from sight, then with a great heave managed to bar their entry once more.

Seating himself on his stool, he shook his head over the mystery presented by Miss Nancy Wright, the newest addition to the Bath Players.

Her speaking voice had that unmistakably cultured tone which indicated she was quality, but Miss Wright had an acting ability he doubted a real lady could ever have. A real lady might be able to play a countess as well as Miss Wright had, but surely no lady could play a saucy scullery maid as well.

Nothing, however, was more mysterious than the way Nancy Wright studiously avoided the many men wishing to meet her. An actress of her beauty could have her pick of wealthy protectors, but she concocted elaborate disguises in order to elude her admirers. Phillips shook his head. Perhaps she was just creating an aura of mystery around her as the jealous Mme Rosa had accused. Perhaps, but Phillips preferred to think she was less calculating than that. He might just be an old man taken in by a lovely smile, but he believed Miss Wright had a very good reason for her behavior, and he, for one, would help her depart unnoticed as long as she wished to do so.

2

The subject of Phillips' thoughts was trudging up-right now that she was out of sight of the theater. The cold, gusty wind chafed her cheeks and penetrated her heavy clothes, lowering further her already drooping spirits. What would she do if Mr. Trevinian fired her? She knew he liked her, admired her acting, and had great hopes for her future, but they both knew she had not had the time to develop her talents enough to play the leading roles. Mr. Trevinian still needed Mme Rosa for the lead, and consequently was likely to bow to her pressure to remove Nancy Wright.

The young woman grimaced as she leaned into the wind and softly damned the increasing popularity that so threatened her livelihood and her anonymity. She had intended to earn her living as quietly as possible. Instead, in a few short months, she had become the new darling of the fashionable young gentlemen of Bath.

A deep shudder shook the young woman's body as she imagined word of the appearance of a new actress with long auburn hair and amber eyes reaching the wilds of Northumberland.

The young woman unconsciously pulled the old pelisse more tightly around her body as her thoughts strayed to the reasons she found herself alone late at night on a cold street far from her home. Home! A small, bitter laugh escaped her. She had no home now, except the small bleak room she rented at Mrs. Ames' boardinghouse. Her father and her guardian had seen to that.

Scarcely had the thought formed in her mind than she gave herself a mental scold. To compare her father, Baron Clemence Spenser, with her guardian, Baron Rudolph Spenser, was as unjust as it was unkind. Her father had only been neglectful, Rudolph had been vindictive.

Catherine Spenser, known in Bath as Nancy Wright, could not blame her father for the love he had held for her mother. Still, she did wish that when his beloved wife had died of a sudden fever, her father might not have lost all interest in his family and estate. Catherine, his only offspring, had been five when her father had turned to the frivolous delights of town to assuage his grief. From the whisperings of the servants, Catherine had long been aware that women were among the distractions her father sought, but from the ledgers of the estate she had learned that games of chance had proven even more beguiling, if less rewarding. When her father died, Catherine, then seventeen, was left with no provision save that which might be made by her distant cousin Rudolph, to whom the entailed estate and title had gone.

Rudolph, when he found he had inherited only empty coffers, had not been inclined toward charity. He had railed bitterly against the old baron and his profligate ways, and then turned malevolent eyes on the old fool's only living relative.

Overnight Catherine's status changed from lady to servant. She was appointed ladys' maid to Rudolph's wife, Leticia, and his two daughters, Dorcas and Hetty; her room was moved to the servants' floor; and she was banished from the family's presence at mealtimes.

Left to her own devices from an early age, Catherine had often eaten with the servants and considered it preferable to eat with her friends rather than her spiteful family. Still, she knew a demotion when she saw one, and she could not help but wonder what would happen next. She had not long to wait.

One afternoon, only a few months after the Rudolph Spensers had taken up residence, not only was Catherine summoned to join the family for tea, she was also sent a new dress to wear. The suspicions raised by the unprecedented kindness only increased when she entered the parlor.

Seated upon the couch with her cousin Rudolph was a heavyset stranger incongruously bedecked in the latest London fashions. Catherine might have laughed aloud at the grotesque picture he made in a blindingly yellow coat and lime-green striped waistcoat had she not been repelled by the look in his eye. She had only read of leers in books, but she knew at once that the look the man had fastened on her decidedly feminine figure was most definitely a leer. The obsequious manner adopted by both Rudolph and Leticia toward the man introduced to her as Mr. Hugo Overstreet, a merchant from Leeds, struck Catherine as like the oily manner of a shopkeeper who is eager to sell a costly item. When her cousin seated her next to the corpulent Mr. Overstreet, Catherine knew she was the costly item.

As she took her seat, she lowered her eyes to hide the anger heating her eyes to gold. It was not that she did not understand the necessity for a marriage of convenience. Her anger arose from her conviction that Rudolph had deliberately sought out the most repellent man possible with whom to unite her. With her head bowed she swore she would not suffer the fate Rudolph had chosen for her. Never would she allow Mr. Overstreet the right to touch her, nor Rudolph such a victory over her.

The next morning when Rudolph had announced with a malicious smile that he had accepted Mr.

Overstreet's suit, she was only surprised at the haste with which she was to be sold. If Rudolph had his way, she would be Mrs. Overstreet in a week's time.

Once in the privacy of her small room, Catherine had immediately begun deliberating the best avenue of escape. She had much less time than she had hoped for, but though Rudolph held most of the cards in their fateful game, Catherine had the advantage of surprise. She was certain that Rudolph would never imagine she was bold enough to flee, nor did he know she had a place to go.

After much thought she hit upon a plan she hoped would work. On Thursdays old Jon, the handyman who had lived on the estate since her grandfather's time, took the wagon into market to sell any extra milk and eggs the estate's cows and chickens produced. To accomplish his task and be home for supper, Jon left before dawn, long before his master and mistress were awake. Catherine knew that, though Jon was now employed by Rudolph, his loyalty was to her. Like all the servants, he doted on Miss Catherine and viewed the changes in her status since the old master's death with great alarm. If Jon conveyed her to the market town, Catherine could use the gold crowns her father had given her on those birthdays he had remembered, to purchase a seat on the stage bound for Bath. In Bath Catherine was certain she would find refuge with her old governess and friend, Althea Reed.

Tears glistened in her eyes when she bid farewell to Lightning, her horse and staunchest friend in the lonely years after her mother's death. But when Jon motioned her into the wagon that Thursday morning, Catherine jumped lightly into the back and covered herself with an old stable blanket. A hundred times on the long, bumpy journey into market Catherine held her breath for fear the voice hailing old Jon was Rudolph's, but her fears proved groundless.

They reached town in time for Catherine to purchase a seat on the coach going south that very day, and in two days' time she arrived dusty and tired on Althea Reed's doorstep.

Catherine grinned to herself as she recalled Allie's look of astonishment. When Catherine was ten, her father had bestirred himself, at the insistent urging of the parson's wife, to provide some necessary, if belated, supervision for his daughter. Relying on the advice of the friend of a friend, he had, quite by chance, hired the perfect companion for his unruly child.

Althea Reed was a sympathetic, intelligent woman who was a teacher as much because she enjoyed her work as because circumstance had forced her to earn her living. Realizing that a child who had had only the supervision of doting servants for five years was unlikely to take well to a strictly regimented schedule, Althea had allowed her charge an unusual amount of freedom. In return Althea had demanded Catherine's undivided attention during the part of the day set aside for lessons. The unorthodox approach had been successful, for Catherine's heart had responded to Althea's kindness and respect, while her quick mind had been equally responsive to the governess's advanced ideas on education.

When after five years Althea had been recalled to Bath to nurse her invalid mother, both pupil and teacher had been heartsore, but at least Althea could console herself with the satisfaction of a job well done. Her charge could discourse intelligently on a wide variety of subjects, and although watercolors had often been neglected for French and needlepoint for Shakespeare, Catherine had, through her association with Althea, developed her innately graceful manner so much that even the parson's wife was heard to exclaim how prettily behaved she was.

Althea had, therefore, been taken aback when a

penniless Catherine had come to her seeking refuge from a loathsome marriage. After hearing Catherine's story, she had been persuaded to aid her former charge, although, with an invalid mother to support, Althea could offer her little more than a cot in her room.

It was enough for Catherine, for she was not the least daunted by the prospect of working. Having successfully eluded Rudolph, she felt free at last to determine her own destiny, and she welcomed employment as a part of her newfound freedom. To her dismay, however, she soon found, as Althea had warned her, that the world was not as ready for her as she was for it. After days and days of futile searching for employment, Catherine's spirits flagged considerably. Without references and possessed of too much youth and beauty for the comfort of respectable matrons, she was denied each position for which she applied.

It was only when she was at her wit's end that providence at last intervened. Passing by the Theatre Royal she chanced to see a circular seeking a young actress to play a role in a Sheridan piece. The idea immediately intrigued her. She had loved the dramas she studied under Allie's tutelage, and had shown a talent for enacting a variety of characters when she and the parson's children put on amateur theatricals.

Althea, appalled by Catherine's "marvelous opportunity," argued earnestly against taking the part, but Catherine was not deterred.

"You needn't be concerned about improper advances," assured the young woman, whose limited experience with men had left her unaware of her physical beauty. "I am sure no one will notice the new actress with only three lines, after all. And, as to my ruining my chances to marry a respectable man, Allie, really, you know respectable young men are not generally in the habit of marrying the governess

or the parlor maid." Seeing that Allie was about to
argue further, Catherine forestalled her. "Oh, Allie,
leave off," she begged, smiling. "I really have no
intention of marrying anyone, so it cannot matter. I
see I have shocked you, my dear, but can you blame
me? My affairs have hardly prospered in their hands
to this point. And besides, how am I to eat? Papa's
sovereigns are nearly gone now."

   Having no response, Allie grudgingly acquiesced
in the scheme and Catherine presented herself to
Mr. Trevinian, who, impressed by her unusual beauty
and intelligence, agreed to hire her despite her inex-
perience. An almost immediate increase in ticket sales
confirmed his decision, and he had kept her on
despite Mme Rosa's increasingly vocal protests.

3

*H*er mind on her troubled thoughts and not on her footing, Catherine caught her toe on the uneven pavement.

"Steady there," a deep, unexpected voice warned as a firm hand saved her from sprawling inelegantly upon the pavement.

In the darkness a startled Catherine could tell little about her rescuer except that he possessed a pair of broad shoulders and was, judging from the fact that she had to lean back to look into his face, very tall. Catherine also noticed that there was an air of elegance about the man's clothing that quite surprised her, for they could hardly be said to be in an elegant area of Bath.

A flash of white teeth answered her shaky thanks and then she heard his voice again. "My pleasure, Miss Wright. I would not want Bath's newest darling to come to harm."

At the sound of her stage name Catherine gasped and tried to pull away from the stranger's hold. "Unhand me, sir," she demanded, becoming more anxious when his grasp tightened.

"Careful there, I mean you no harm." The stranger was well-spoken, his voice low. He may have meant to be soothing, but he sounded like he was trying to gentle a horse to Catherine, and she was having none of it.

"I am not accustomed to being accosted by strangers. Let me go," she insisted.

Quite suddenly the wind gusted heavily. It whipped at the gentleman's greatcoat and caused Catherine to stumble toward him. When a great fork of lightning lit the skies and was followed by a deafening crack of thunder, the stranger leaned down to shout into her ear.

"Miss Wright, you mistake me. I have a position I wish to offer you. A position as an actress," he added as he felt her stiffen. "Come, there is an inn around the corner where we may find some privacy."

Without giving her a moment to reply, the stranger moved in the direction he had indicated, keeping his hold on Catherine's arm.

A drenching rain began to fall in the wake of the thunder, and Catherine, sheltered somewhat by the gentleman's large figure, felt little inclination to pull away. He had made mention of an offer of employment, and with Mme Rosa's words still ringing in her ears, she had reason enough to listen to him.

Within a few moments Catherine found herself standing before a roaring fire in a pleasant private room in the inn the gentleman had mentioned. The innkeeper, though he eyed the figure of the hag somewhat dubiously, was all smiles and bows for the imposing gentleman, who rapidly fired off a list of demands in a decidedly authoritative manner.

While the stranger was giving their host his order, Catherine had the opportunity to study him from under the brim of her bonnet. He had removed his beaver hat and his greatcoat to reveal thick black hair that curled slightly over his well-shaped brow. His nose was straight—aristocratic, Catherine thought—and his mouth looked generous without being too full. Judging from the grooves beside his mouth and his air of command, she guessed he was around thirty years of age.

The fit of his coat of blue superfine was so exquisite over his broad shoulders and narrow waist that Catherine did not doubt it had been ordered from one of the best London tailors. A snowy-white cravat was tied in a faultless style with which Catherine was not familiar, but which was far more elegant than the absurdly fussy ones sported by the dandies at the theater. Her gaze moved lower and she noted that the gentleman's buckskin breeches fit tightly over well-muscled thighs, while a pair of Hessian boots, shiny despite the rain, completed his picture of sartorial perfection. It was a bit daunting to Catherine to realize that never in her life had she seen such a handsome man.

"Do you approve, Miss Wright?"

The stranger's amused voice recalled her abruptly to her manners, and though she blushed to be caught staring, Catherine managed to give him a direct look. Fortunately for Catherine, her months of working as an actress had given her some control of her expression, or she might have disgraced herself completely when her eyes met the stranger's, for his were a most startling silver-gray. Staring out from his swarthy countenance and surrounded by ridiculously long black lashes, they were quite the most compelling eyes Catherine had ever seen.

Seeing the stranger's mouth quirk slightly, Catherine guessed he knew to a nicety the effect his appearance was having on her. Well, she thought, he would soon learn she was not some simpering miss, swayed entirely by a gentleman's appearance. This man had some accounting to do before she could remain alone with him—no matter how persuasive his looks might be.

"Forgive me for staring so, sir. We are not accustomed to such elegance in this area of Bath. I would know who you are and what your concern with me is."

"A practical woman, I see," the stranger replied with a slight smile curving the corner of his well-formed mouth.

Catherine was not pleased by that smile, which she thought condescending in the extreme. Her chin lifted in an eloquent, unspoken reply.

"Allow me to present myself, Miss Wright." The stranger's bow mocked her. "I am Adam Edward Charles Vincent Beaufort Cameron, Duke of Clarendon, Earl of Wrexton and Bougher, and on and on and on."

This time Catherine could not control a gasp of amazement. "What on earth can be your business with me?" she asked, her tone both wary and incredulous.

"As I said earlier, I have, er, a, role for you, but before we get to that, it occurs to me that I have been most remiss as a host. Surely you would be more comfortable without those things on."

Catherine was in no mood to have her clothes derided as "things." Her "things" had saved her from the unwanted attentions of unscrupulous rakes, of whom she was still not certain this disconcertingly attractive man was not one, and she was not at all certain she should part with them until she had heard his business. However, before she could inform him that she would keep her "things" on, thank you, their host entered the room, followed by a young lackey carrying a tray on which there was a bottle of port, a pot of tea, and a plate of steaming meat pies whose savory aroma soon filled the room.

It happened that Catherine could rarely eat before a performance, and on this day she had not eaten since noon, nearly twelve hours before. When the aroma of the pies wafted about the room, her stomach began to rumble loudly. So loudly, in fact, that when the innkeeper and his boy had left and silence had settled once more upon the room, Catherine was sure the duke must hear it. The thought that he might think her too poor to feed herself galled her, and she realized that, unless she was to listen to his offer of employment while holding her stomach, there was nothing for her to do but help herself to at least one of those tempting pies.

With unconscious grace she shed her wet garments, laying them upon a chair, and moved toward the table, where the duke stood holding out a chair. She saw that he was regarding her with a twinkle in his silver eyes, as if he guessed exactly what her quandary was and why it had been resolved as it had. Just as she thought to make a tart observation on the unfortunate effects of hunger, a subject of which she thought the duke was certain to know very little, her stomach gave a mighty and prolonged growl. She was dismayed, and her eyes flew to his face. There was no reaction, his expression was quite bland. The gallantry of his effort, for Catherine had no doubt he had heard the indelicate sound, won her gratitude, and she grinned ruefully at him.

"I fear I must apologize for the most improper squawking of my stomach, but these pies have proved too tempting by far."

As Mr. Phillips could have warned the duke, Miss Wright's smile, especially when her beguiling dimple appeared, was very powerful stuff. Having seen Miss Wright only from a seat in the audience, Clarendon was quite unprepared for its effect at this close range. He recovered quickly, however, and returned her smile with a modest one of his own.

"There is no need to apologize, Miss Wright, I understand completely that few actors are able to eat before a performance."

So saying, he waved her to her seat and served her a pie as well as a cup of tea. While she proceeded to do justice to the delicious pies, he helped himself to port.

"Allow me to congratulate you on your perform-ance, Miss Wright. Your talent stands out quite distinctly in that mediocre company."

Her mouth full, Catherine merely nodded, though a vision of Mme Rosa swelled to the bursting point with indignation caused a smile to tug at the corners of her mouth.

"I hope you shall not let Madame Rosa hear that assessment, your grace, for she would not be the least bit pleased I can assure you."

Taking another bite of her pie as she said this, Catherine missed the satisfied look that briefly crossed her companion's face.

"Madame Rosa does have a reputation for being jealous of popular, young actresses," he remarked. "And I would guess that tonight must have been a particular trial to her patience. Those young bucks stopped the performance at least twelve times to applaud you."

His words were met with what could only be termed an exasperated snort. "I confess I cannot really blame her," Catherine said when she had swallowed her mouthful. "It is most difficult to stay in a role when the dialogue is being stopped continually by idle young men vying to see who can make the most racket."

The duke's dark eyebrows lifted in surprise at this statement, though Catherine was once again too busy with her repast to notice. More than a little familiar with the species actress, he had never met one who did not hunger for acclaim. Either this one was un-believably naïve, or she was monstrously sly, knowing exactly what to say to create a picture of earnest innocence. The duke's eyes narrowed cynically as he watched the young woman help herself to another piece of pie. Innocence and the theater were hardly synonymous.

"Their applause is meant to recognize your beauty

and, mercifully, in your case, at least, talent," he said, having his reasons for humoring her.

Catherine stopped eating long enough to mutter darkly, "I thought as much. No doubt they carry on that way regardless of the actress's talent?"

"Indeed, ma'am," was the laconic reply. "In fact, I attended a play once where the dandies clapped loudly in spite of the fact that the actress forgot half of her lines. She forgot them so prettily, however, she brought the house down."

Catherine searched her companion's startling eyes for an indication of the truth of his story. A slight quirk of his expressive mouth intrigued her. "You must be teasing me," she said more as question than as statement.

With an air of exaggerated injury the duke replied. "Well, she did bring down the pit."

Catherine giggled at the absurdity of his manner, and he found himself grinning back, his eyes on her dimple. Her eyes were on his smile. Gone was his arrogant, mocking expression. In its place was a devastatingly boyish one. She realized, after a moment and with no little embarrassment, that she was holding her breath, and letting it out with a rush, she spoke quickly to divert attention from her bemused manner.

"Whether you are teasing me or not, I am sure some such outrageous thing has happened. I think it is a great shame that those who are actually interested in drama must sit through such unseemly interruptions." Under her breath Catherine added, "Which are a great deal of trouble, besides."

"I beg your pardon?" the duke inquired politely.

"Nothing, your grace. I only wondered if you are going to eat this piece of pie. It is the last one," Catherine said, her sense of honor forcing her to enlighten the duke, though her stomach was still eager for more.

The duke observed the reluctance with which his young companion forced herself to point out the importance of the lone piece of pie, as well as the undoubtedly hopeful look in the large amber eyes raised up to him. Finding himself quite diverted by those oddly colored eyes, he reassured her with an easy gesture. "They were all meant for you, Miss Wright. I have already eaten. But perhaps you would care for more?"

Having eaten three moderately large pieces of pie and about to begin on her fourth, Catherine felt the twinkle in her companion's eye to be lamentably justified.

"If I had another piece, I would be too mortified for words," she observed candidly. "I am afraid I shall just have to make due with four pieces and a cup of tea."

The duke laughed aloud at that, though he did admonish her not to let pride stand in the way of making herself truly comfortable.

She assured him she really was quite full. Indeed, now that she had finished the delicious pies, was on her second cup of tea, and was ensconced in a warm, cozy room, Catherine realized she hadn't been so comfortable in days. The instant the thought formed in her mind, it was countered by an alarm. Whatever was she thinking? she scolded herself. This man was a total stranger whose intent might well be to lull her into a false sense of security. Catherine cleared her throat and tried to look as daunting as possible.

"It is time, I think, that you told me about the employment you mentioned earlier."

The duke watched the play of emotions on Miss Wright's beautiful face and was amused by her attempt to look severe. He was tempted to tease her further until thought of his business with her sobered him. With a gravity of manner she had not seen before, he suggested she take a seat by the fire.

"You might as well make yourself comfortable, Miss Wright, for my story is neither pretty nor short."

After she was seated, her eyes were drawn to her companion as he stared into the fire. Neither his body nor his face looked like those of the Earl of Warwick, the only really exalted nobleman she had ever seen. On a trip to Alnwick Castle, Althea had pointed him out, and Catherine remembered now how his soft, pudgy body had spoken of indolence and his pasty complexion of sheltering indoors. He had looked toward the little knot of visitors with the silliest expression, too, a sort of sneering petulance that had made Catherine giggle.

This man's body was nothing like that. Taut, muscled, and lean, it bespoke hard use, and the brown of his skin testified to how little time the Duke of Clarendon spent indoors. But it was his face that looked the least like the effeminate earl's. Its sharp angles and the way his lids sometimes closed halfway over his startling eyes gave him a closed, ruthless look. He looked more like a startlingly handsome highwayman or pirate than a noble, like a man who had seen a great deal and had taken what he wanted along the way.

With an abrupt, impatient gesture the object of her scrutiny turned to look at her, an incongruously apologetic smile on his face. "Forgive me the delay in starting my story, Miss Wright. Now that I am at the point, I hardly know where to begin." He shrugged his broad shoulders lightly, then settled his back comfortably against the mantel. Looking sometimes at Catherine and sometimes at his glass of port, the duke began speaking again in his low voice. "I suppose I should just begin at the beginning. And in the beginning, I was the second son. It was my older brother, Gerald, who inherited the title when our parents died several years ago." He nodded absently in response to Catherine's murmur of sympathy. "Gerald and I had always been close, and our loss deepened the bond. Though he was a bit young to be my guardian, we managed well enough with the assistance of our aunt, Lady Emily de Maine. Our lives were normal enough, and when he left the university, Gerald returned home to tend the estates, while I, after my university days were over, went up to London to acquire some town bronze."

The duke paused to take a drink of his port, and Catherine wondered if she had imagined a deepening of his ironic tone as he mentioned his early years in London. When he resumed speaking, however, his tone was even once more.

"Eventually I made myself useful by joining Wellington on the Peninsula. It was just as my third year came to an end that I received word from home that Gerald had died in a riding accident."

A look so bleak passed across the duke's face that Catherine's heart went out to him. She felt an impulse to touch him, to recall him from the pain of his loss, but she realized from the closed look on his face that he would not relish such an intrusion. Instead, she watched the expression on his face change slowly from one of sadness to one of great bitterness.

"As soon as I could, I returned home to mind the family fortunes and to investigate Gerald's sudden and, to my mind at least, mysterious death. Now, Miss Wright, you will need to know that Gerald was the best rider in the county. Knowing that, you will appreciate my astonishment when I was assured by the magistrate that Gerald was thrown when his horse shied for no apparent reason—as if Gerald had not been managing startled horses since he was in short pants."

The duke's eyes were as cold as icy shards when he dismissed the official explanation of his brother's death. Catherine, observing that look, thought inconsequentially that his grace would not be a man to cross.

"What is your opinion, your grace?" she asked, breaking the uneasy silence that had fallen.

"Murder," was the reply said so softly the hairs on Catherine's neck raised. In response to Catherine's involuntary gasp of astonishment the duke swung around, fixing her with a penetrating look. "Oh, yes, I know. It's impossible. No one goes around killing peers of the realm. And God knows Gerald had no enemies. I've gone over it all a hundred times in the year since I've been home. There are no gambling debts, no cuckolded husbands, nothing. Unlike his younger brother, Gerald was the very pattern card of respectability."

The duke struck the mantel with his fist. "Someone was clever enough to make his murder look like a simple riding accident, but I swear he will not get away with it!" He pulled a chair close to Catherine. "Which brings me to you, Miss Wright," he said, fixing her once again with his compelling eyes.

Fascinated, Catherine sat erect in her chair, her attention riveted on that silver gaze.

"Since there seems to be no personal reason for his murder, I have begun to think that the motive may be connected to the estate. I believe someone is trying to get his hands on the Cameron wealth. If that is true, then it follows that I am next."

Despite his grim expression, the duke's manner was calm, and Catherine found herself accepting his fantastic observation that he was a target for murder in much the same spirit.

"Who stands to benefit the most, your grace?"

The duke nodded, as if pleased with her response. "Eustace, my nephew and heir, is the first person to come to mind. However, I am not yet convinced of his guilt."

The duke fell silent, studying the tip of his boot a

moment. His heavy lids were again closed halfway over his eyes, recalling to Catherine's mind the image of a lethal bird of prey.

"Still," he resumed, his soft tones menacing, "someone is my enemy. Fortunately, unlike Gerald, I am aware of my danger, and I intend to use my knowledge as an opportunity to trap the man. I have decided to force his hand by announcing my betrothal. It is my guess he will decide to act against me before the day of my supposed marriage in order to save himself the trouble of having to murder my son."

The duke paused again, and Catherine was suddenly aware of the wind hurling rain against the inn, the logs crackling as they were consumed by the fire, and her own heart beating quickly. This time when her companion lifted his gaze to hers, the look, though still intent, was lightened somewhat by a small smile playing at the corners of his mouth.

"Have you guessed your part, Miss Wright?" he asked softly. "Will you consent to act the part of my betrothed?"

Catherine expelled the breath she had not realized she was holding. At his mention of a betrothal, she had indeed formed some idea of his intent, but she was nonetheless nonplussed by the extraordinary request.

"You are taken aback," her companion said easily. "But I assure you I am not mad, and what's more, I shall make the masquerade well worth your efforts. Two thousand pounds will be settled upon you when the villain is captured or at the end of a year's time, whichever comes first."

"Two thousand pounds," Catherine repeated.

"Two thousand," he confirmed. "And you have nothing to lose. No matter what happens, you will earn that sum and in the meantime live a life of fashion in London."

Catherine said nothing, merely turning to stare

into the fire, unaware that the duke's hooded eyes watched her. She could understand his reasoning. A betrothal would likely force the culprit's hand, and for a man like the duke, any action would be preferable to waiting for his enemy to make the first move.

But . . . Catherine's mind reeled with objections to the scheme. First and foremost was her concern that she could not possibly pass muster as a future duchess. Not only would there be family and friends to convince, but Catherine had a shrewd idea that the Duke of Clarendon was a figure of note among the *ton*. She would have to withstand the scrutiny of the members of the highest circle in England every hour of the day for perhaps as long as a year. It was too much.

"I sympathize with your grief, your grace, and I understand the motives behind your plan. However, I cannot, despite the considerable benefits involved, accept your proposal. I believe you would be wasting your money and my time. All society would have to accept that you had passed over all the suitable young women of your acquaintance to choose a completely unknown young woman to be your future duchess. As we say in the theater, it just would not play."

When he spoke, Catherine was very much aware that the eyes behind the heavy lids had grown cool. "Miss Wright, you are an actress, and therefore, not overly familiar with the *ton*. I am, and I suggest you leave it to me to decide what will or will not be accepted by society."

Catherine's own temper was sparked by what she considered an arrogant dismissal of her legitimate concerns, but reading correctly the flash in her amber eyes, the duke raised his hand, forestalling her angry retort.

"Modesty is, I am told, a virtue, Miss Wright, but you go too far. One look at you—dressed in fine feathers, of course—and no one will question my choice." Catherine was not given the time to savor the compliment, for her companion continued speaking in clipped tones. "And there are few who would dare to criticize me. They'll all want to be on good terms with my future duchess, never fear. Besides, as I'm rich as Croesus, no one will wonder why I did not hang out for an heiress. I may marry where it takes my fancy to do so, and every one knows it—I daresay expects it."

Though she longed to administer a set-down to such unmitigated arrogance, Catherine did not. It was obvious this man could and would do just as he pleased and be congratulated for it where lesser mortals would be censored. The force of his personality was such, Catherine thought wryly, that if he chose to marry a milkmaid, he would start a rage for country lasses. He was regarding her now from beneath his heavy lids with a rather tolerant air, as if he expected he could command her as he did the *ton*. But, unlike the *ton*, Catherine was still not convinced of his grace's superior judgment.

"I concede your superior knowledge of your social circle, your grace," she allowed. "However, there is yet a flaw in your plan. I am new to acting, and I still find it a difficult challenge to play a part whose every word is written and every gesture directed beforehand. To play the role you suggest over the extended period of time you have mentioned would require knowledge of a hundred nuances of polite behavior of which I know nothing—or next to nothing." Catherine added scrupulously, the years of Althea's tutelage in her mind. "I would bring the whole thing crashing about your ears."

"Miss Wright," the duke began—and Catherine was immediately aware of the impatience in his voice—"you may trust my judgment. I have been looking about for a suitable actress since last November, and

I have settled upon you. You played a countess to perfection in that play two months ago."

Catherine's eyes widened in surprise.

"You see, I have been quite thorough," he mocked. Catherine could almost hear him adding "as always" beneath his breath, before he continued with his persuasion. "There is an air of quality about you: the way you hold yourself, the way you move, and most important, the way you speak ... I don't suppose you know if you're from the wrong side of some aristocratic blanket?"

The outrageous question elicited an exclamation of shock. "My family history is none of your business," Catherine blurted indignantly. "But I assure you that I am not ..."

Catherine's brief tirade ground to a halt when she could not bring herself to say what she was not.

"A bastard?" the duke finished helpfully, the boyish grin on his face evidence of his amusement at Catherine's delicacy.

"Your grace!" Catherine flared, the flush on her cheeks turning crimson in mute testimony to her embarrassment.

The duke stared at his companion, thinking she seemed as shocked by his language as any schoolroom chit might have been. Perhaps she was as naïve as she appeared. He bowed his apologies. "I did not expect you to be quite so sensitive," he explained.

"I see," Catherine said, seeing very well that the duke thought an actress would think nothing of being called a bastard.

The duke did not give her time to dwell on his unfortunate words or the unrepetant twinkle in his eye, however, for he continued, "At any rate, any little niceties of manner you may lack can be supplied by Aunt Emily, Lady de Maine. She makes her home with me in London and, as when I was young, tries very hard to mother me."

The thought of anyone trying to mother this assured, arrogant man caused Catherine's mood to veer from indignation to amusement. It seemed rather like the hen trying to tame the fox.

The duke evidently read her response in her eyes, for he quirked an expressive brow at her. "Just so, Miss Wright. It has been a difficult, even frustrating task, and she shall be in raptures to have a girl to dote on. She has been after me since my return from Spain to settle down with some simpering miss. You will seem a godsend to her—my salvation at last."

Beneath the ironic tone, Catherine detected a genuine warmth of feeling toward Lady de Maine. Her discovery caused her to moderate her opinion of the man before her. Evidently he was not always so arrogant and domineering.

"But surely you would tell your aunt of your masquerade?" she asked doubtfully.

"No, indeed," was the astounding reply.

"But . . ." Catherine began.

Before she could continue, she felt the full effects of the duke's most thunderous frown, a frown that had been known to send even highborn dowagers into a quake. "Miss Wright, may I remind you that I believe my life is in danger? Though I regret deceiving Aunt Emily, I believe it necessary to bring a murderer to justice."

Catherine flushed at the rebuke. "I understand, your grace. I did not intend to impugn your motives."

"Just my methods?" the duke asked dryly. Catherine flushed again at the mockery in his all too perceptive eyes, but was spared the necessity of making an answer when he shrugged as if dismissing an unimportant matter. "Your understanding is not important, but your participation is, Miss Wright. Have you decided to accept my offer?"

Catherine steeled herself to bear more of her perspective employer's anger. She had not yet decided to accept, and she would not be browbeaten into accepting something she should not.

"I do have one or two more questions, your grace. Is there no one with whom you have formed an attachment? Someone who might feel betrayed by your betrothal to a stranger?" Catherine hoped to defuse the anger she guessed her question might generate by looking as ingenuous as possible. She honestly did not meant to be disrespectful, but she also knew she could not possibly accept a position that would cause a great deal of heartache for another.

"I thought I had made it plain that this matter is far more important than the temporarily ruffled feathers of some female or other," the duke snapped, apparently not the least mollified by Catherine's purposefully wide-eyed look. "Nor can I imagine what business it is of yours. I am asking you to be an actress, not my confessor. However, I suppose it is no great concession to tell you what half the world knows. No, Miss Wright, there is no one expecting to marry me, if that is what you meant. I have been quite adept at avoiding any matrimonial snares."

Catherine was aware that the duke had answered only half her question. If there was no young woman of the *ton* whose heart might be broken, might there not be a mistress who would be discomfitted to learn of his impending marriage? A quick look at the closed expression on his face convinced her it was not an important question.

Instead, she asked, "I believe it most unlikely, your grace, but what would you do if I were recognized?"

"In that extremely unlikely event I would simply say I didn't care a fig if you were nothing but a mere actress, I still intended to marry you. A few doors might close to you, but I would be betrothed. That is all that matters."

Catherine scarcely heard the duke's explanation. She was stunned by the careless disdain he had dis-

played. It was not just the words "mere actress," but
the tone of voice he had used as well. He was not
trying to be impolite, she realized; he had merely
been giving voice to a widespread attitude: actresses
were irrevocably beyond the bounds of polite society.
Though she had encountered some of this attitude in
the six months she had been an actress, she had
never felt such an acute sense of dismay as she now
experienced. All actresses were equally disreputable
as far as the Duke of Clarendon was concerned, and
Catherine, without a by-your-leave, was condemned
along with all the rest. A surge of anger served to
rout the completely unexpected jab of pain she experienced. Who was he, with his lineage and wealth
handed to him to judge her, after all?

"Are there other questions you wish to put to me,
Miss Wright?" The duke was looking at her with a
frown.

"No, your grace. I can think of no other questions." Catherine managed with great effort to keep
her voice level. "However, I cannot possibly make a
decision tonight. Your proposal is a most unusual
one, and will require some careful consideration."

The duke had been scrutinizing her face closely,
and despite Catherine's even voice, he could tell from
the gold spark in her eyes and the defiant set of her
soft mouth that she was angry. It did not please him
in the least that for some elusive reason the chit was
making him wait on her decision. There was little he
could do about it, but his cool voice testified to his
displeasure. "As you wish, Miss Wright. You will
understand that I wish to put my plan into action as
soon as possible. Would tomorrow morning be sufficient time for you to come to a decision?"

Catherine nodded, her manner as formal as his. "I
think I can decide by then. If I do accept, when had
you planned to leave for London?"

"The following day," he replied.

"But that is scarcely time to give my notice or to buy the proper clothing," Catherine objected.

"We shall avail ourselves of Aunt Emily's sense of fashion in London." The duke's tone dismissed that aspect of her objection as absurd. "As to the theater, if Trevinian will not release you, I shall buy out your contract, although considering Madame Rosa's attitude, I doubt it will be necessary."

Catherine spent the few minutes it took to put on her pelisse and bonnet fuming silently. Not only had she been described as beyond the pale of polite society, but she had then been informed as well that she did not have the sense to see to her own wardrobe. The man was impossible, insufferable, and insensitive!

When an hour later Catherine sat on her narrow bed in Mrs. Ames' boardinghouse, she almost had to pinch herself to be convinced the evening had not been a dream. The experience had been so unusual, the emotions she had experienced so varied and in some cases so new, she could scarcely believe she had not imagined it all.

Even the short walk home had been rendered by the duke's presence extraordinary. He had insisted on accompanying her in tones so final she had not argued the need twice, and she had been keenly aware of his presence at her side. Once, when she was blown backward by a particularly strong gust and the duke's arm had closed about her waist to steady her, a bewildering surge of warmth had coursed through her body, causing her to fairly jump from his touch. It did not ease her confusion that, although the winds had been howling loudly at the time, Catherine was fairly certain she had heard a deep chuckle issue from her companion.

And now, Catherine wondered, what was Miss Wright to do? Put herself in the hands of an arrogant, condescending nobleman or remain at the mercy of Mme Rosa? There was not much choice. With the

two thousand pounds she and Althea could realize a
dream they had of living in a pretty cottage in the
country. Althea had a cousin with just such a place
on his farm near Winchester. Nor would Rudolph be
likely to look for her in a duke's house in London.
She could hide from her guardian and have a taste
of fashionable life at the same time.

With the assistance of the duke's aunt, she thought
she could do reasonably well with the part. The duke
could give it out that she was from the country, and
though her manners might not be as polished as
some in the duke's circles, they would certainly pass
as those of a country girl of good family. After all,
that was what she was—whatever the Duke of Clarendon might think!

And now she had come to the real reason for her
hesitation: her employer. The Duke of Clarendon
was a very attractive man who thought of her as a
useful but lower order of being. She deeply resented
his unmerited judgment and was not at all sure she
wished to live with it day in and day out. She did
have to allow that he was unbelievably attractive, but
that was all the more reason to stay quite clear of
him. Her cheeks burned when she recalled the feeling she had experienced when his arm had encircled
her.

After a few minutes Catherine's pensive look faded
into an impish grin. Wouldn't it be fun, in addition
to earning two thousand pounds, seeing justice done,
and playing a real-life duchess, in addition to all
that, to teach her arrogant employer that not all
actresses could be dismissed as "mere." Some, or at
least one, was as intelligent and worthy as anyone in
his exalted circles, and she would make him admit it.

4

Next morning when the sun struck her eyes, Catherine did not, as usual, bury her head beneath the pillow to sleep on uninterrupted. Instead, a sleepy smile crossed her face. The sun, heralding the end of the blustery weather, seemed a good omen. Surely nothing terribly ill-fated could begin on such a day.

In the breakfast room, Allie, already seated with a plate of kidneys and eggs before her, looked up surprised when Catherine entered.

"Good morning, Allie," Catherine greeted her friend, her amber eyes sparkling with excitement. "I have the most astonishing news you will scarcely credit it! After my performance last evening, I chanced to meet the most exalted lord who made me, well, a most interesting proposition." Catherine studiously ignored Allie's shocked gasp. "And it is so, ah, lucrative, I simply cannot afford to decline."

"Catherine," Allie shrieked.

Smothering her laughter Catherine dreamily tipped her head to one side. "I shall have fine clothes, jewels, perhaps a carriage . . ."

"Catherine Spenser!" Allie's body was a stiff line. "I do believe you are funnin' me, but I can tell something has quite excited you. Now, stop your teasing and tell me what it is."

Catherine laughed, a sunny, carefree laugh that could enchant and could, as now, bring an answering smile to the listener's face.

"Oh, Allie, you should have seen your face! Forgive me for teasing you, I couldn't resist. And before you poker up again, let me tell you that all I have said is true, though it is not as you imagine it to be."

Althea's response, after Catherine's explanation of Clarendon's proposal, was hardly less shocked than before.

"But, my dear, this is extraordinary! How do you know this man really is the Duke of Clarendon? I have heard of the family, of course. Who in England has not? But Catherine, love, you have no proof of his identity. Perhaps he has devised this story to win your sympathy and to use you for his own purposes."

Reflecting as she sipped her tea that Clarendon's arrogant assurance could only belong by right of birth to a man whose ancestors had been prominent since the Conqueror had stepped on England's shores, Catherine responded at last in forgivably wry tones, "I think you will be convinced of Clarendon's identity when you meet him, Allie."

A peremptory knock sounded at the front door, and soon after, Mrs. Ames' broad figure appeared, her cheeks flushed with excitement at having such an obvious member of the nobility in her boardinghouse. One look at Catherine, however, recalled the probable reason such a nobleman might have for visiting an actress, and Mrs. Ames' excitement visibly diminished.

"There's a right smart gentleman come to call on you, Miss Catherine, but no matter how important he may be, I'll not be havin' anything sinful happenin' in my house."

Before Mrs. Ames could launch into a recitation on the iniquities of actresses, a subject on which Catherine was feeling particularly sensitive, she stood. "Miss Althea is joining me, Mrs. Ames. The sanctity of your boardinghouse shall remain quite unimpaired." Her sharp tone did little to appease the landlady, but Mrs. Ames stood aside as Althea followed Catherine toward the parlor.

If the duke found it surprising that an actress was chaperoned, he did not indicate it by so much as the flicker of a drooping eyelid, greeting Althea with faultless courtesy. Catherine was amused to note Allie's dazzled response, though she could not blame her for it.

Clarendon looked every inch the Corinthian this morning. His bottle-green coat and buckskin breeches, though subdued in color, were of the finest materials and fit his hard, lean body like a glove. His cravat was again elegant without being absurd, and his Hessian boots bespoke the services of a meticulous valet. That same valet had neatly brushed the duke's dark hair back from his forehead, though one lock, evidently no more biddable than he, had escaped to fall onto his brow. In the light of day Catherine saw that the duke's gray eyes were even more silver in color than they had looked the night before.

"I must say, Miss Wright, that you look much improved this morning." Catherine with great effort did not flush at his amused perusal of her simple dress. "You will forgive me for saying it is a welcome change from the drab I met last night?"

"You are forgiven, your grace." Catherine was pleased with the collected tone of her voice. "The old drab is, after all, meant to repel." Turning to Allie, Catherine explained that she had disguised herself as an old crone. "Through some undisclosed means"—she arched a delicate brow toward the duke—"his grace managed to penetrate my disguise."

He shrugged innocently. "Such loveliness as yours, Miss Wright, could not remain hidden from the truly discerning observer, no matter the disguise."

It was a pretty compliment, but by reminding herself that it was also an effective dodge of her question, Catherine was able to prevent a pleased blush from heating her cheeks, even going so far as to tell herself that eventually she would be able to receive such praise without the merest flicker of an eyelid, no matter if the speaker were the odiously handsome man who stood observing her with such an amused air.

When the duke addressed her again, however, all amusement had faded from his countenance. "I know haste is unfashionable, Miss Wright, but I am sure you will forgive me, as you are aware of my special situation. Have you had sufficient time to reach a decision?"

With a steady voice, Catherine decided her future. "Yes, your grace, I have decided to accept your proposal." Her eyes were on his as she spoke, and when the duke smiled a smile of pure, open delight in response to her words, Catherine felt a physical jolt.

"Splendid," he replied. "I am delighted to hear it. I am positive you shall not regret your decision."

"Do you still wish to leave tomorrow, your grace?"

"I do. Will Trevinian let you go so abruptly?"

"I think he will," Catherine replied, worrying her lip while she considered the best way to handle the theater manager. "There is an understudy for my part, of course, and I suspect Mr. Trevinian will not be entirely devastated to see her take my place. A respite from Madame Rosa's harangues should be welcome compensation for the loss of Nancy Wright."

"He'll find himself without patrons, if he continues to defer to her," Althea observed angrily. "She has entirely forsaken acting for posturing."

Catherine grinned at her friend's indignation on her behalf. "Where is your Christian charity, Allie?" she teased. "I hear desperation in her tirades. Madame Rosa is growing older without having put away much money to support herself in her old age."

Seated opposite the two women, the duke took

advantage of the crowded room and Catherine's attention to Allie to study his newest emloyee.

With the eye of a connoisseur, he noted that although her blue merino dress would be considered shockingly plain by any fashionable lady, its soft material showed to advantage the pleasing curves of Catherine's slender body. He was particularly relieved to see that her face was as free of paints as it had been in her role as hag and that her petal-soft skin needed none. Her dark-chestnut hair was likewise seen to better effect in the light of day, its red highlights gleaming in the sunlight. Only her expressive eyes and her soft, full lips looked much the same as they had the night before.

With a start Clarendon realized she was addressing him, and he further realized that he, rather than taking stock of the faults as well as the merits of his employee, had been staring like a schoolboy.

"What story shall we tell in London?" he asked, recovering.

Hearing the curtness of his tone, Catherine glanced at him sharply. She wondered if she had offended him somehow; perhaps her teasing manner with Allie was too familiar for such a nonpareil. It was difficult to read those cool, veiled eyes, however. An unbidden thought occurred then: would his expression be so inscrutable, if one knew him well . . . quite well? The thought was repressed as quickly as it had surfaced. It was only an idle thought anyway, she certainly would never know him that well.

"We will say," his voice recalled her to the matter at hand, "that we met in Wales, I've a remote estate there. We don't need any parents, so yours will have died in an accident—a boating one, perhaps—and you will have been living with the local parson, who was a close friend of your family. We'll give you the name 'Asterley.' There were some Asterleys near the estate who did die rather suddenly a few years ago.

It is not entirely unlikely that they may have had a daughter. At any rate, the area is so remote and uninhabited as to guarantee we shall not encounter anyone who could deny our fabrication. As to your first name, I believe I overheard the landlady address you as Miss Catherine. I vastly prefer it to Nancy and require that you will use it. You shall be Catherine Asterley."

The imperious tone in which her employer commanded her to use her name sparked Catherine's by no means small flame of rebellion. He could at least have asked if Catherine Asterley met with her approval!

"Catherine Asterley is most satisfactory. I accept it," she said after a telling pause. "There is one other matter, however, your grace," she added sweetly. "Miss Asterley would have a companion for her trip. I do hope you have made arrangements for someone to join us on our journey."

A sudden gleam in the duke's eyes seemed to indicate he was aware of the indignation his arbitrary manner had provoked and was amused. "I had hoped you would be able to provide an appropriate companion of your own," he replied easily, inclining a questioning brow toward Althea, who explained that she could not leave her invalid mother.

"I see. In that case I shall take my leave so that I may devote my day to assuring you of your respectability, Miss, ah, Asterley."

Clarendon rose at once to go, then turned suddenly, only missing a large shelf of figurines by inches. "By the bye, what time do you leave for the theater this evening?"

"At five o'clock," Catherine answered, a question in her eyes.

"My carriage will be here to transport you and to return you after the performance."

"Oh, your grace, there is no need of that," Catherine protested.

"Perhaps, but you shall avail yourself of its security nonetheless. I do not want a cutpurse dashing my scheme at its inception," he informed her coolly.

Unable to deny that she would be safer riding in a carriage than walking, Catherine accepted the duke's pronouncement with as good grace as possible.

"As you wish, your grace," she replied, looking with casual unconcern at her fingertips and thus missing the twinkle her forced compliance brought to the observant gray eyes.

"What an impossibly arrogant man!" Catherine expelled the words as soon as the duke had departed. "Ordering me to use his carriage whether I wanted to or not, and not for my sake, at all, but only to protect his precious plot."

"He does seem quite accustomed to having his own way, but I suppose that is all part of being a Cameron and a duke." Althea looked with concern at Catherine. Left alone with only loving servants to act as a curb, her former charge had grown up very much accustomed to her own way as well.

"Do you think you can contrive to tolerate the duke for the length of time it will take to resolve his mystery?"

Catherine's eyes darkened as she considered Allie's question. She truly did not know the answer. She had not forgotten the tone of voice in which he had said "mere actress," although he had never behaved so condescendingly today. If he returned to that attitude, she would, indeed, find it difficult to get on with him. Further compounding her uncertainty was the bewildering variety of emotions she had experienced since first encountering the duke a mere twelve hours ago. Sympathy, excitement, anger, and a host of other emotions she could not even name, all seemed to be swirling about inside her, completely obscuring any clear view of the man.

"I do find him perplexing," she said finally. "However, our goal is rather more important than any annoyance we may feel with each other. I think we can contrive to rub along somehow."

5

"May I present Margaret O'Malley?"

The duke's carriage had just departed from Mrs. Ames' boardinghouse, and Catherine was meeting the third member of their party, a short, plump girl with large, round, brown eyes and curly black hair peeping out from a frilly maid's cap. Had she herself hired her maid, Catherine knew she could have done no better than this fresh-faced young woman. Clarendon might be top-lofty, but he was not insensitive, for he evidently understood that Catherine would need a friendly ally to serve her while she maintained her pose as his betrothed.

Catherine looked more closely at the brown eyes gazing at her apprehensively. They strongly reminded her of a puppy who has been ill-treated and anticipates the same harsh treatment with each new master.

"I am pleased to meet you, Margaret." Catherine smiled at the timid girl. "You shall have to help me a great deal, you know. I've never had a lady's maid, so you will have to teach me what you should do. I daresay it's unusual for the maid to tell the mistress what's expected, but you look very capable, and I'm sure I shall be a credit to you in no time."

Margaret's eyes darted quickly from Catherine to the duke. Evidently the slight smile quirking his mouth reassured her, and with a real, though small, smile of her own she replied hesitantly, "It will be my pleasure to serve as beautiful a lady as you, miss."

Unsatisfied with so hesitant a response, Catherine persevered. "You are very kind to say so, Margaret, thank you. However, I should think how I behave will be even more important to you. I promise to try to remember I am only a mere actress and not a highborn lady who looks at you like this." Her eyes sparkling irresistibly with mischief, Catherine sucked in her cheeks and lifted her nose high in the air in perfect imitation of a haughty dowager for whom servants were quite beneath notice.

This time Peg smiled broadly. "La, miss, but you did look just like some ladies as I've seen." Then, two bright spots appearing on her cheeks—apparently because she dared to say more—she cleared her throat. "But, miss, I am usually called Peg, not Margaret, miss."

"And so you prefer Peg?" Catherine asked. When Peg's head bobbed yes in reply, Catherine nodded in return. "Then Peg it is," she confirmed with a smile.

Throughout her exchange with the little maid, Catherine had been aware of the duke lounging on the seat opposite her, his long legs encased in gleaming Hessians stretching to her side. She had seen from the corner of her eye the flash of his white teeth in response to her mimicry, and it had been all she could do not to turn to catch that devastating smile. Telling herself her reaction to him was due solely to the fact that he was the first exceedingly handsome man she had ever met, she thanked him graciously for finding her such a perfect companion.

"I am glad you approve my choice," he replied to Catherine's thanks. Then in a lazy drawl he added after a pause, "I trust you had an uneventful trip to and from the theater, Miss Asterley?"

The amused mockery in his voice lifted Catherine's chin a notch. "Quite so, your grace. Your stratagem may commence quite unhindered."

"So much warmer than tramping about in the chill

night air, too," said Clarendon, all innocent, if persistent, amiability.

"And your carriage is much softer on the feet than are the cobblestones," Catherine agreed coolly, looking away as if the matter bored her.

When the duke gave a great shout of laughter, however, Catherine's haughty pose disintegrated and her face dimpled with a mischievous smile.

"Come, admit, you were glad to have the carriage," he said, his eyes on that smile.

"I do, I was," she agreed readily. "But I do not like to be told so peremptorily what I will be doing. You must moderate your commanding manner, your grace, if we are to rub along happily together."

Catherine heard Peg draw in a breath at this presumption, but kept her eyes steadily on her employer.

That gentleman, his hooded eyes revealing little of his reaction, only replied easily, "Perhaps we can settle on a compromise. You are, I hope, familiar with the word?"

His light manner was met with a gurgle of laughter. "Yes, your grace, although more in theory than practice, I am afraid. I was forever being rebuked for my stubbornness as a child, but I shall endeavor to meet you halfway in our dealings."

"Good," said her employer with a satisfied air. "There will of necessity be instructions on how to behave in society, and we do not have the time to wage a war over each request."

"I have said I will be guided by reasonable requests." Catherine's chin went up again as she felt it necessary to stress the word "reasonable" before she lost complete control of her life.

"And," continued her companion, blandly ignoring her bristling reply, "I wonder if you have heard the word 'demure' in your circles, Miss Asterley?"

Catherine's eyebrows shot up at the obvious irony

in the question. "I do not believe I have given you
reason to think me forward!"

"I assure you, Miss Asterley, that no properly behaved young lady would walk unchaperoned into
the private room of an inn with a complete stranger."

"Oh!" Catherine's eyes widened at the memory.
There had been the storm, her need for a new
position, and his arm on hers, but none of that
signified. She had not hesitated. What must he think
of her! "You are correct, your grace," she admitted,
lowering her head in remorse. "I shall in future be
more circumspect."

The duke regarded the color staining Catherine's
delicate cheekbones from beneath his lids for several
moments. Apparently unsatisfied, he lifted her chin
with a long elegant finger, forcing her amber eyes
up.

"There's no need to be so penitent, *chérie*," he
drawled, half-amused. "My words are for your good
as well as mine. London is much larger and more
fraught with danger than Bath."

When her chin was released, Catherine turned to
stare unseeing out the window, suddenly remembering a conversation she had had earlier that day. Allie
had pleaded with her to tell Clarendon her real
identity. "I am concerned," she had said, "that he
will treat you in a manner unsuited to your upbring-
ing. He believes you to be an actress and the Lord
knows what he thinks of them."

Catherine, knowing quite well what the duke
thought of actresses, had still disagreed. "If he knew
I were gently bred, he would not hire me. Even the
high and mighty Duke of Clarendon could not pay a
proper lady to pretend to be betrothed to him. Only
a cad would consider bringing a 'good' girl so low.
It's all foolishness, of course. Gently bred or not, I
need to eat. However, I am persuaded Clarendon
would have nothing to do with what he would term a

compromising situation. No, Allie, I am certain that if I tell his grace who I really am, he will decide to look for another actress, and after giving my notice to Trevinian, I cannot afford that."

At this moment Catherine did not feel so certain she was right. Perhaps she should explain who she was, tell him she had gone with him because she was a green girl, not a loose woman. She did not, however, prevented again by the fear that she would lose her much-needed employment.

6

After a brief stop for luncheon Clarendon had abandoned the ladies to ride ahead on his stallion, Ares. His departure left Catherine and Peg free to become better acquainted, and to Catherine's relief, Peg, without the duke's presence to intimidate her, had shed much of her awestruck manner and proved to be a delightful chatterbox. Nevertheless, it had been a long day and Catherine sighed gratefully when their inn came into sight. It would be heaven just to stretch.

That she could not resist searching the busy innyard for the duke she excused on the grounds that the sooner he was found, the sooner she would be released. What purpose this explanation gave the footman proceeding toward the door was uncertain and remained unaddressed, as at that moment Catherine caught sight of her employer, his broad shoulders and height dominating those about him. He walked toward the carriage with a lithe, effortless sort of grace that Catherine had never had the privilege of witnessing before, but instinctively sensed would draw the attention of women. Watching him, she wondered if it was a personal attribute or one cultivated by all men of fashion.

"I trust your journey was pleasant," the duke inquired politely as he handed her down.

Catherine smiled as he led her across the yard, dodging the ostlers, horses, and dogs that filled it.

"Indeed, your grace, it was a very pleasant journey. Who could doubt it when you provide such a luxurious carriage?"

The duke caught the mischievous twinkle in the look slanted at him. "So much more enjoyable than walking, you would agree?" he asked, a trace of lazy laughter threading the question.

Her voice laden with exaggerated dismay, Catherine nodded. "I fear you may have ruined me altogether, your grace. I declare I may never be able to revive my taste for walking again."

There was a slight pause while the duke cast Catherine an enigmatic glance. "I daresay luxuries are easy to become accustomed to."

Catherine intended to make a pert response but was forestalled by the appearance of the innkeeper. It was Catherine's first opportunity to observe at close hand how the world treated a duke, and privately she thought it little wonder that Clarendon was so top-lofty, if the bowing and scraping done by their host was an example of how most people behaved toward him.

The innkeeper's wife personally escorted Catherine and Peg to their rooms, promising to send along hot water and tea "in an instant, milady."

The duke remained below, watching Catherine climb the stairs with narrowed eyes. One moment the chit was posing as an innocent and the next she seemed to be hinting at a desire to become his mistress. Tired of walking, indeed! A mocking smile curved his mouth. Whether she had done it on purpose or not, he rather thought those words had revealed her true colors. He had met very few women who wouldn't sell themselves for luxuries like his carriage.

Completely unaware that she had left her employer with such a dubious impression of her motives, Catherine prepared eagerly for dinner, and although she was hungry, she was also honest enough to admit that a dinner with Peg would not have caused her heart to skip a beat.

The little maid wound her gleaming auburn hair into a smooth knot pinned at the nape of her neck, then with expert fingers picked out several long tendrils, setting them free to curl becomingly around her mistress's face.

The gold taffeta she donned had been her mother's. Althea, with minimal assistance from Catherine, had modernized it, and Catherine thought it emphasized her hair and eyes nicely enough to descend to dinner with confidence.

At the bottom of the steps, she encountered the innkeeper's wife, who showed her to a private dinning room down the hallway. The duke, there before her, stood at the fire idly nudging a recalcitrant log with the toe of his boot. Even without the aid of his valet, who had been sent on to London with word of their imminent arrival, he looked formidably elegant in an impeccable coat and a snow-white neckcloth. By comparison, Catherine's taffeta looked hopelessly shabby.

To make matters worse, Catherine saw a table set for two. What little assurance had been left her after comparing her ensemble to his deserted her completely. How could she, who had scarcely socialized with any men other than the parson and his young sons, be expected to entertain a gentleman alone? And not just any gentleman—a particularly exalted, handsome, and rapier-sharp one to boot!

The duke turned around to find his employee looking quite young and hesitant as she hovered by the door, her large eyes looking a deep-honey color as they darted anxiously from him to the table. Whatever her plans for the future might be, he thought with a wry lift of his brow, it did not seem the chit's past was filled with much experience.

Pulling himself from his thoughts, Clarendon set about putting Catherine at ease, for it would not do to give her a fright of her social abilities. Two of the qualities she needed most were poise and charming manners, if he was to convince the world this girl was, indeed, his choice for a wife.

"You look quite charming, by the by," he remarked after bidding her good evening and settling her by the fire. His offhand drawl somehow reassured Catherine more than an effusive compliment might have done, and she was able to reply with a smile.

"Thank you, your grace, you are very generous. I am afraid my skills with a needle cannot compare with those of Weston, however." Her gaze dropped enviously to the duke's superbly tailored coat.

Her employer could not resist smiling at her expression, though, once again he guessed she was hinting at something else.

"It makes no matter what you wear, you would look charming in almost anything," he assured her easily.

Catherine tried to smile a calm, unruffled acceptance of the compliment. Despite her effort, however, she could feel the telltale heat in her cheeks. Adding to her discomfort was the oddly speculative look she could detect in the heavy-lidded gray eyes observing her so closely.

The entrance of two maids with their dinner broke the odd moment, and when they settled to enjoy a delicious roast duck, Catherine felt relaxed enough to ask the duke if he would tell her what to expect in London.

He complied, informing her, among other things, that a young miss was not allowed to dance the waltz unless approval to do so had been secured from one

of the hostesses of the exclusive club. Almack's. She
learned who these hostesses were and was vastly entertained when the duke mimicked their haughty
airs. She was told a young miss might have lemonade
or ratafia, but would be considered fast if she par-
took of more than a glass of champagne. She already
knew—but did not reveal that she knew—that young
ladies must never allude to portions of the human,
particularly male human, anatomy by more than the
vaguest of euphemisms, and that she must never
allow even the most seemingly innocent familiarity
from any gentleman lest she be thought fast. Although the sheer number of rules was staggering,
Catherine made no fuss about them, for they all
seemed either reasonable enough or too trivial to be
worth bothering over. However, the final injunction—
that under no circumstances was she to speak on
anything other than the most bland of topics (he
even suggested the weather!)—was disappointing.
Catherine had looked forward to conversing with
people whose minds were as exalted as their rank.

"But is anyone ever serious about anything important?" she asked with a frown.

"Not often," replied her mentor in amused tones.
"It is considered bad *ton* to know or care anything
about anything more important than the cut of your
clothes, the origin of your snuff, and the genealogy
of your cattle." Looking closely at his crestfallen employee, the duke asked with a slight smile, "Not a
bluestocking in disguise, are you, Miss Asterley?"

Catherine laughed, though her eyes remained
thoughtful. "Nothing so frightful, your grace. You
forget, however, that unlike the *ton*, I have seen
another side of life, where everything is not always
pleasant. I wonder who will see to the terrible condi-
tions in our mills, or assist the poor soldiers who
come home from Boney's wars without more than a

by-your-leave for their lost legs and arms, if not the most privileged in our society?"

The duke's brow arched in surprise. "Who, indeed? Such sentiments are, if surprising in one so young, to your credit, Catherine. However, I do not exaggerate. Were you to give voice to them, you would be considered 'not quite the thing,' and our business calls for you to be accepted with as little comment as possible. Do you understand me?"

"Yes, your grace." Catherine gave a sigh of exaggerated penitence. "I shall do my best to present myself as a butterfly fluttering mindlessly from one entertainment to the next."

The duke's intent manner lightened slightly at her flippant answer. "I cannot think you will be too sorely put out by your obligation," he observed dryly.

"Well, I suppose it is not such an onerous task," Catherine conceded, her dimple peeping out.

When their host entered to supervise the clearing of their supper, Catherine rose from the table feeling the evening was going better than she could have hoped. The duke had been most charming and gracious, and she began to feel more confident about the next few months. However, there was one subject on which she still needed reassurance, and she raised it when they were seated by the fire.

"Will you indulge me, your grace, if I confess to one particularly large concern?"

When the duke merely nodded, Catherine continued. "Although I am anxious about my reception among the *ton*, it is your aunt, Lady de Maine, who concerns me the most. I find it difficult to believe that she will be willing to accept a provincial nobody as your future bride."

The duke stretched his long legs toward the fire and settled himself comfortably before answering. "I suppose your concern over Aunt Emily is understandable," he conceded in his deep voice. "Perhaps you will have to meet her before you are able to accept the truth of what I say. But to please you," he said, throwing her an ironic glance, which brought an answering smile from her, "I shall give it a try."

He explained that his aunt, unable to have her own children, had showered her sister's two children with all her love. When her husband died only a year after the duke's parents had passed away, Gerald had suggested she take up residence at Clarendon House in London and act as his hostess. As the arrangement suited Adam also, Lady de Maine had remained.

"She has always bemoaned the fact that there were only a pair of rugged scamps to look after. I cannot say how strongly I believe she will be delighted to distraction to have the opportunity to fuss over a girl."

Catherine smiled rather weakly, still a little dubious about his aunt's reception.

"Am I to understand by that weak excuse for a smile that you are doubting me again? I assure you, my girl, I have spent a great deal of time finding someone who would be acceptable as my betrothed. Your beauty and your charming manner will combine to win her, you will see."

The stern tone in which the duke uttered his assurance robbed it of its flattery. Indeed, the almost quelling look on his face seemed to indicate annoyance that Catherine should dare to remain so unsure. After all, had not he approved her first?

Catherine could not help but grin at his haughty look. "Please forgive me for doubting the quality of your standards, your grace. I will strive to remember that if you approve, the world can do little better than to follow."

A lazy smile quirked the duke's lips. "Minx," he chided, a fascinating gleam in his gray eyes. "But I am pleased to see you take my point. I am sure you will be readily accepted."

"I do have one other question, your grace."

Clarendon raised his eyes to the ceiling as if to ask for patience from heaven, but Catherine, aware of the smile lingering in his eyes, felt free to continue.

"I have been wondering how you plan to be rid of me in the end?"

The duke waved his hand in a dismissing gesture. "When we have discovered the identity of our culprit, we shall decide what to do. If you wish to continue your career, we shall disclose our scheme. On the other hand, if you wish to retire from the stage, we may simply invent a fatal illness for you."

"Something painless, I hope." Catherine smiled.

"Have you any thought as to which course you would prefer to follow?" the duke asked. "Is there a young man whom you wish to marry rather than continue your stage career?" He observed with interest the shadowed look that very briefly dimmed Catherine's vivid eyes.

"No, your grace, there is no young man," she said in a voice that held a faint and, he thought, unconscious trace of bitterness.

Intrigued, the duke persisted. "It is difficult to imagine a girl as lovely as you without a single suitor. Is there some dreadful secret that I should know?"

Catherine smiled, although a sudden image of Mr. Hugo Overstreet made it a very fleeting one. "No, nothing dreadful. I was raised in a rather isolated area, and there were no young men about. Well, there was a six-year-old, a ten-year-old, and a thirteen-year-old, but no one of a more reasonable age."

"Very isolated, indeed. Where . . ."

Unfortunately, Catherine had overlooked the need to create a history for herself, and knowing she could not invent a satisfactory one on the spot, she seized the first idea that came to her to divert the duke's interest, saying, "Besides, I am not interested in marriage. Putting myself entirely in the hands of another person is repugnant."

"Marriage is repugnant?" quizzed the duke, thoroughly diverted. "I thought all young women yearned to marry. No, I've got it—you are an original and desire instead to be a mistress so that you may maintain your independence."

"I do not! That would be demeaning," Catherine yelped, stunned at the turn the conversation had taken.

"And marriage repugnant? You have sworn off men altogether then, my dear. Now I do wonder if you know all that you are discarding so lightly?"

Catherine's eyes widened at the soft, almost silky sound of the last words. A new look, one even she, as inexperienced as she was, recognized as dangerous had appeared in the duke's eyes.

Accordingly, she set her glass down upon the table. "It has been a most pleasant evening, your grace," she addressed the duke's shoulder after rising. "However, riding, even in your well sprung carriage, is fatiguing, and I beg you will excuse me."

To her utter consternation the duke leaned his dark head back and let out a shout of laughter. "You'll do famously in London, Catherine. Your instincts are unerringly proper. So you hope to flee the rest of this conversation, do you?"

"I think it has gone as far as it should go," Catherine responded evenly, though her heartbeat quickened when the duke rose from his chair and walked toward her.

Not wishing to seem a coward, Catherine fought her instinct to run and stood her ground. It was an unwise decision. Her employer halted so close to her that she was made acutely aware of just how caressing his silver-gray eyes could be.

"Such a pity to deprive mankind of so lovely a

prize," he said quietly, never taking his eyes from hers.

Catherine, caught fast by that searing look, could not move. When the duke's strong hand moved to softly caress the pulse beating frantically at the base of her throat, Catherine shivered despite the extraordinary warmth of her skin.

"Your grace!" She at last found the strength to stumble from his touch, her cheeks stinging with heat. "Please, I must retire," she whispered before fleeing the room.

Next morning Catherine felt little inclination to face her employer. She had acted, she burned with shame to recall, like a rabbit held captive by the cannier, more powerful fox. How could she respond so when she knew he only dallied with her, a "mere actress"? Fool, she blasted herself as she descended to breakfast.

To her immense relief the innkeeper's wife informed her that his grace had already breakfasted and gone to check on the horses. Sunshine poured into the breakfast nook, and while Catherine sipped her tea, she soothed herself by reflecting that her reaction to her employer's caresses was no doubt why society insisted young women be chaperoned at all times. Surely she was not so lost to all modesty as she had feared. Besides, she had a shrewd idea that her employer was a particularly effective assaulter of virtue.

Catherine giggled as a ludicrous picture of the duke, outfitted with grappling hooks, preparing for an attack on the H.M.S. *Chastity*, rose in her mind.

"Well, Miss Asterley, if you are laughing over you own thoughts at breakfast, I believe I can presume your sleep was most, ah, restful."

Catherine swung about, startled by the sudden appearance of the object of her thoughts. He looked impeccable as always, while she, dressed in her alternate day dress, a simple green woolen thing, looked, she had little doubt, a complete dowd.

"I rested very well, thank you," she replied stiffly. "And you, your grace?" she asked, determined to behave in an ordinary fashion.

"Oh, I suppose I rested well enough, though"—and here the Duke's mouth curved wickedly—"I was a bit lonely."

Once again Catherine felt charmed almost against her will. A twinkle she could not hide lightened her lovely eyes to gold.

"Fancy that," she answered in mock surprise. "I would have thought that after all these years"—her emphasis was dramatic—"you might have grown accustomed to life without your nanny."

"You wound me, Miss Asterley." White teeth flashed in her companion's dark face. "I am sure this is a malicious reference to my advanced age. No doubt you are trying to put me in my place?"

Catherine, having already risen, moved toward the door. With her hand upon the latch, she tossed her employer a saucy grin. "Not at all, your grace, you mistake me entirely. I am merely trying to keep you out of mine."

The words said, Catherine made immediately for the safety of the hallway, where she smiled delightedly upon hearing a deep chuckle issue from the private dining room.

7

"There are so many people!" Catherine's wide eyes looked out the carriage, feasting themselves on the wondrous sights afforded by her first glimpse of the capital. Her senses were assaulted by the riot of colors and smells. And the noise! There was a bewildering cacophony of sounds issuing from the hordes of people as some hawked their wares, others bargained for those wares, and some merely heckled the passersby.

"Whatever is that man doing?" Catherine asked for perhaps the tenth time in many minutes.

The duke, who had abandoned Ares on the outskirts of London, replied that the man was a streetside orator, "hoping to save a soul while making a ha'penny, I imagine." An elegant brow arched ironically as the duke continued, "Did I fail to mention, Miss Asterley, that an excess of emotion is considered most unseemly in polite society?"

Catherine tore her eyes from the fascinating scene beyond the window to flash a speaking glance at her employer. "And no doubt polite society is as accustomed to visiting London as are you, your grace. Never having had such an opportunity myself, I find it far too marvelous to contain myself."

The duke's mouth twitched ever so slightly, and seeing it, Catherine grinned beguilingly. "Can we come to a compromise, perhaps, your grace? If you will only allow me to be Miss Wright a few moments

61

longer, I promise I shall be the fashionably languid Miss Asterley forever after."

Taking in the sparkle that had turned her eyes to gold, the duke replied with lazy self-interest. "I doubt it will be necessary to entirely leave Miss Wright behind. And yes, my dear, that dome yonder really is St. Paul's."

At last the carriage reached quieter neighborhoods, where the homes became gradually larger. When it turned into the drive of a particularly imposing mansion, Catherine caught her breath. When she was faced with this confirmation of her employer's wealth and consequence, her excitement was replaced by a distinct fluttering in her stomach.

"Ah, I see Davies has spotted our arrival." The duke had stepped down and was reaching up to assist her. For an instant Catherine hesitated, unable to move.

"Catherine?" The duke's voice was polite though firm, and Catherine realized there was nothing for it but to take his hand and become Catherine Asterley, his betrothed.

Emerging from the mansion's door as they ascended the steps was an erect, white-haired woman of medium height, dressed in a fashionable, blue silk gown.

"Adam! Oh, Adam! I received your message only yesterday." She embraced the duke warmly, then turned to Catherine with a welcoming smile on her lips. "My child, I am Emily de Maine, Adam's aunt. And you must be Catherine, for you are as lovely as Adam promised."

Catherine murmured a response, she scarcely knew what, and was ushered into the house. Nervous though she was, it did not escape her notice that Lady de Maine's gray eyes, so like the duke's in color, were giving her a shrewd look of assessment.

Once inside, it was an effort for Catherine to keep

her attention on her hostess, however, for all she wanted to do was to gape at the magnificence around her. The size of the hallway, the elegant, fashionable furnishings, the scores of quiet, liveried servants, all combined to convey an impression of old, limitless wealth.

Davies, the butler, was particularly awe-inspiring. When, a haughty expression on his long, drooping face, the old retainer bowed with exactly the correct degree of angle to his presumably soon-to-be mistress, Catherine had to resist an impulse to curtsy. Worse, when she caught a gleam of amusement in the duke's eye, she found she had to stifle an equally unsuitable impulse to giggle. Looking quickly away from the duke's unsteadying influence, Catherine managed a gracious smile and, sternly subduing her desire to gawk, gave her attention to Lady de Maine.

"I know you must be fatigued after such a long journey, my dear," the duke's aunt was saying. "If you like, you may go at once to your room for a rest. I have ordered some tea, though, if you feel up to joining me for a cup?"

"Thank you, my lady." Catherine smiled. "That would be most pleasant. I fear I am such a country bumpkin that seeing the marvelous sights of the city has quite revitalized me."

Lady de Maine clapped her hands together in a little gesture of pleasure. "Oh, I am so pleased you enjoyed your arrival. So often people from the country are afraid of all the noise and the crowds. Adam"—she turned to address her nephew—"Mr. Terry has been waiting breathlessly for your arrival. He insists he must see you, though why such a supposedly astute man of business cannot wait until you have had a cup of tea is beyond me. I promised I would send you along, however, so I suppose I must. You needn't worry about Catherine at any rate; we'll have a nice coze without you."

The duke looked at Catherine, who had to suppress a cowardly urge to beg him to stay, and smiled. It was such an encouraging smile, she found herself returning it.

"Until tea, then, my dear?" he asked.

Catherine nodded. "Until tea," she confirmed and, taking a deep breath, bravely followed Lady de Maine up the sweeping staircase to a large saloon on the next floor. Catherine's eyes lit when she entered, her fears temporarily forgotten as she surveyed the room's graceful mahogany furniture and rich Aubusson rugs. The pleasure of such lovely surroundings was a delightful and unlooked-for benefit to her employment.

"I hope you will call me Aunt Emily, Catherine," Lady de Maine spoke from behind her. "I want very much for us to be on the best of terms."

Catherine turned to look closely at the duke's aunt, for she was not yet convinced her cordial greeting was sincere. The expression in lady de Maine's gray eyes, however, was convincingly earnest. Touched, Catherine answered a trifle shyly that she would be pleased to call her Aunt Emily. "I have always wanted an aunt," she said, hesitating before she confided with a worried smile that appealed to Lady de Maine's warm heart, "I only hope I shall not be a trial to you. I warn you I shall need a great deal of instruction on how to go on properly."

"Nonsense, my girl!" Lady de Maine smiled broadly. "I shall be in alt to show you about."

After a slight pause Lady de Maine spoke again, the shrewd look Catherine had noted earlier reappearing. "I wonder, my dear, if you are also concerned that I may be disappointed because Adam has not selected a girl from a family of the *ton*?"

Catherine, masking her surprise at such directness, replied in the same spirit. "It is of concern to me, my lady. Surely you must have wished for a better match for your nephew."

Lady de Maine took Catherine's hand in hers and leaned forward as if to stress the sincerity of her next words. "My first and only concern is for Adam, Catherine. I had hoped, after Gerald's death, that he would settle down. Alas, he has seldom been inclined to heed my advice, and this time was no exception. I am afraid you will learn that Adam has led very close to a rake's life. He does take, I am glad to say, his duties on his estates most seriously, but when in London he has . . . My dear, I am speaking so plainly I hope you aren't shocked."

Vastly more intrigued than shocked by Lady de Maine's interesting and not entirely surprising revelations, Catherine merely murmured that she welcomed plain speaking when it was necessary.

"Oh, I am relieved, because I do want you to understand my feelings in this matter quite clearly. I do believe we will become friends so much more quickly if we do not have any doubts between us." Recollecting where she had left off, Lady de Maine continued, her expression lighter. "Suffice it to say no eligible young woman has ever caught Adam's interest, though countless ones have tried. And that is why, my dear, I am so grateful to you. It is time Adam found a woman who can share his life. And with such a beautiful bride—no don't blush, it is only the truth—I am persuaded he will soon be providing a proper heir just as he should do."

The arrival of an elaborate tea tray punctuated Lady de Maine's triumphant summation of her hopes for the duke's future. During the lull in conversation that occurred while the tray was settled and Lady de Maine poured, Catherine was given an unwanted opportunity to savor the sour taste of guilt. Face to face with such sincere hopes, Catherine's conscience shrank from the part she played in raising them so falsely.

Still wrestling with her doubts, Catherine glanced

up to see the duke enter, looking as unruffled as an innocent babe. Irritably she thought how easy it was for him to be so sure of himself while she was left to bear, all alone, the burden of his aunt's fool's paradise.

"Rest easy, Aunt Emily," Catherine said, an impish impulse making her turn an ever-so-innocent smile up to his grace, "your nephew has spoken fondly of the children he hopes to have. Haven't you, my dear?"

If she had hoped to lighten the burden of her guilt by making him share it, she failed. The duke, appearing not the least disconcerted, gave her a lazy grin. "With you to inspire me, my dear heart, I certainly do look forward to the, ah, opportunity to have many children.'

Catherine blushed scarlet at his words, and the pulse at the base of her throat began beating in the same frantic way it had the night before.

"Adam, you incorrigible boy, you have put this darling girl to the blush!" Lady de Maine leapt to her defense. "I fear I shall have to apologize for him, Catherine. He's always resisted my attempts to civilize him, but I did think he could get through tea without making any impertinent remarks."

Catherine's embarrassment succumbed to amusement as she observed the quelling glare the slight Lady de Maine turned upon her nephew. "Please do not apologize, Aunt Emily." She even was able to smile. "As I have already become acquainted with your nephew's character, I assure you I am accustomed to his manners."

The duke's brow lifted in ironic acknowledgment of her words. "I see I have no alternative but to beg your pardon, my dear. I own, however, that I do not actually feel remorse for bringing such a pretty blush to your fair cheeks."

Even as Catherine felt a new blush rising, she strove to remember that the duke's role called for

him to bestow such flattery on her. His words were
meant more for Lady de Maine's ears than hers.
With that thought in mind, she was able to respond
lightly, "Such fair words call for a fair pardon, sir.
You are forgiven."

Lady de Maine had been watching their exchange
with a pleased smile. "Wild you may be, Adam, but
you are sweet-tongued as well, which such a dear girl
deserves. But never mind all of this cooing! We have
vastly more important matters to discuss. Catherine
and I will not have much time for you over the next
several days, for we will be quite taken up with shopping. Suzette is prepared for us to come to her
tomorrow and swears she can have several things
ready by Tuesday. That is the day of Joanna Enderby's
soiree, which would be a perfect time to present
Catherine. There will be a relatively small though
select gathering, not the overwhelming crush we might
encounter at a ball or rout."

The unrestrained relish with which the duke's aunt
was planning their affairs brought a smile to Catherine's lips, and glancing up, she found an answering
smile on her employer's dark, handsome face. He
raised a brow as if to say, "I told you so," and
Catherine bowed her head in acknowledgment. Her
fears about Lady de Maine had proven to be as
unwarranted as he had tried to tell her.

After tea Lady de Maine showed her to a light airy
bedroom decorated in shades of blue where Peg was
waiting, her brown eyes glowing. When Lady de
Maine departed, the little maid could no longer contain her excitement. "Even the staff act grand, Miss
Catherine," she declared. "Still, grand or no, they're
as nosy as can be about you. It seems most of 'em
thought his grace might never marry." The expression on her face conveyed shock, whether in reaction
to the idea of anyone not marrying or this attractive
nobleman in particular, Catherine could neither guess

nor ask, as Peg hurried on. "The maids said he'd
suffered a broken heart long ago and had decided
having dozens of mistresses was better than taking a
wife. They're all pleased that he's going to give up
his wild ways now, especially with you bein' as lovely
a sight as you are."

While she rested, Catherine could not help but
wonder whom the duke had loved and why the
woman had left him. She found it difficult to imagine any woman willingly giving up Adam Cameron.
Nor could she resist wondering if he really had had
scores of mistresses. Lady de Maine had seemed to
imply as much. After a moment Catherine shrugged
her graceful shoulders, exasperated with herself. The
duke's broken heart—if he had one—and his other,
rumored affairs were no business of hers. She was
merely his employee.

8

*T*hree days later Catherine, though she ached from head to toe, felt like Cinderella. Lady de Maine, in her role as fairy godmother, had whisked Catherine from one shop to the next, scarcely pausing for rest, and had accumulated in the process enough clothes, as Catherine incredulously informed her, for an army of people.

While she was being turned into a young lady of the highest fashion, she had seen little of her employer. He had dined with them once, but otherwise he had been absent, saying only that he was enjoying his last moments of freedom before their social rounds began. "Catherine understands," he had assured his aunt, flicking Catherine a glance.

She read her cue and dutifully said she did, which was true. With no new person for whom to play the betrothed couple, the duke had decided his time would be more amusingly spent with his friends, or his mistress perhaps, than with her. She only wished she were more relieved by his absence. The evenings with Lady de Maine, delightful as that lady was, were somehow lacking, and Catherine could not prevent herself wondering where the duke went and what he did when he got there.

But this afternoon she knew she was to see him, for he had relayed a message through Lady de Maine that his Aunt Honorine and her son and the duke's heir, Eustace, were coming to tea. Luckily, or perhaps the duke had arranged it in his commanding way, the first of her dresses had arrived from the dressmaker. Catherine donned the jonquil sprigged-muslin eagerly, pleased to appear in something so becoming, and with a light heart tripped down the stairs to do a little pirouette before a smiling Lady de Maine.

"Behold! I am quite transformed." She laughed infectiously. "I am now the fashionable rather than the dowdy Catherine Asterley, thanks to you, ma'am."

Lady de Maine chuckled with her. "I accept your thanks, love, though I fancy you and Suzette have more to do with the pretty picture you make than do I."

As Catherine moved to take her seat, she caught a movement at the door and, looking toward it, saw the duke was there, leaning negligently against it, his eyes fastened on her. For a long moment their eyes held and Catherine could not find the strength to look away. He was looking at her so strangely, she thought, he must have seen her silly behavior over her new dress and think her quite childish.

"Adam!" Lady de Maine's voice broke between them.

Watching her employer stride over to place a kiss on his aunt's cheek, Catherine noted again the languid grace with which he moved. She knew now, having seen many on the street, that few, if any, London gentlemen moved with that particular ease, and that few looked even half so compelling.

"What do you think of our efforts?" Lady de Maine waved her hand at Catherine, who waited more anxiously than she wished for his verdict. Earlier she had thought her dress, with its capped sleeves and soft material, delightful, but now, faced with her employer's close scrutiny, she had doubts. Surely it made her look a little young, a sophisticated man like the duke. . . .

"Delightful," he pronounced before Catherine lost her nerve entirely. Raising her hand to his lips, he added more softly, "Though it scarcely does justice to the wearer."

A blush suffused her cheeks, but she grinned at him. "You are too kind, your grace. I only hope you will not regret your words when you discover the extent of the wardrobe Aunt Emily has decreed I must have. I vow there are no clothes left in London after our assault."

"Tut! Tut! Adam don't want his duchess looking' like a rag doll. Your concern with cost is most vulgar, Catherine," Lady de Maine sniffed in mock affront. "Tell her, Adam, that she must not protest even a little when I order the two new pelisses I believe she really must have."

"Aunt Emily!" Catherine protested, laughing. "I cannot imagine where I shall wear all of the pelisses we have already purchased. Two more and I shall imagine you want me out of the house at all times, you will have prepared me so well for the out-of-doors."

"Aunt Emily is in the right, Catherine. She knows what you need," the duke intervened, regarding Catherine with an odd, speculative look before he added more lightly, "Besides, it is a most agreeable pleasure to see you look so charming."

"You see," Lady de Maine crowed, not allowing Catherine a moment to savor the duke's words. "I told you, my girl. And we'll have no more of your penny-pinching, or I shall personally buy you a dozen more pelisses."

Catherine laughed outright at the older woman's fond teasing, throwing up her hands in defeat. "I swear to surrender to your judgment from this moment forward."

A knock at the door interrupted them, followed by Davies, who, in a tone so grave he might have been announcing the fall of the exchange, informed Lady de Maine that Frenier, the duke's French chef, wished urgently to consult with her.

"Might as well go down now," Lady de Maine grumbled. "No doubt his feathers are ruffled because I've asked him to fix the lamb in an English style. Why he cannot realize he now lives in England, not that dreadful France. . . ."

Lady de Maine's aggrieved voice trailed off as she left to attend to the matter.

"Your grace," Catherine immediately addressed her employer. "There is something I must ask you while we are alone."

"Oh?" her employer queried.

"Yes, you see, you haven't been here much, and so you probably do not realize, but . . ." Catherine bit her lip, trying to think how best to put the matter. She did not think the duke, having discussed the issue once, would be thrilled to have it raised again. "Aunt Emily," she began again more slowly, "has become my friend, you see, and I know now how terribly disappointed she will be when she learns the truth about our betrothal. I hate this lying to her. Could we not tell her the truth? She would support you in anything you wished to do, I know."

The duke did not reply, but stood staring almost broodingly at her. Catherine bore his silence for a bit, but when she decided he intended to ignore her altogether, her patience snapped.

"I deserve a response!" She glared at him hotly. "And I wish you to quit looking at me in that way."

"In what way?" asked the duke, his drawl maddeningly lazy.

"As if I were a species of strange plant you've just discovered and are trying to determine whether or not it is poisonous," Catherine retorted in a decidedly unlazy fashion.

A wicked grin curved his lips. "I'd never mistake

you for a plant, my dear," he said, his eyes sweeping over her.

Catherine flushed at the look in his eye, but noted to herself that he had not actually dismissed the fancy that she might be poisonous.

"I suppose I do find it curious that you actually seem to care for Aunt Emily." The duke's words were said so softly, Catherine wasn't sure she'd heard him correctly. Before she could ask what he meant, he continued. "As to telling her about our scheme, I think not."

"But . . ." Catherine's eyes eloquently pleaded her case.

The duke's expression softened a bit before her earnestness. "It is difficult for me to play her such a trick as well, Catherine. Believe me, if I could, I would do this another way. But she is too transparent. Her friends would smell a rat, and our quarry, whoever he is, might get wind of it and lay low. The only advantage I have is that no one suspects my betrothal to be a deception. I cannot take the chance of losing that advantage by including Aunt Emily in the secret."

Catherine considered his answer for several moments, finally inclining her burnished head in a grudging nod. "I suppose I must agree, though I cannot like it."

"Our first compromise, my dear. We should toast it with something more substantial than tea. Nor was it so difficult to achieve. I believe your detractors were speaking libel when they called you stubborn."

Catherine laughed up at him, her eyes lighting up in the most delightful way. "There is no compromise to toast, as you well know. You've won the day entirely and for very good reasons, I allow. Still, you must admit that I am the one who must face Aunt Emily while you are able to hide away in your club or wherever it is you go."

"Ah," the duke exclaimed softly, an arrested look in his eyes. "Dare I hope you have felt a trifle neglected? I had thought that, feeling as you do about men, you would be glad to see less of me, but. . . ."

"Not at all," Catherine said as airily and as quickly as possible. Too late she had heard the reproachful note in her voice, and now she must live down a knowing gleam and a twitching mouth. "I only meant that I must listen more than you to your aunt's plans for the future, and it hurts me to know how useless they are. However, as you have made your decision, I do not see the purpose in discussing the matter further."

"My dears"—Lady de Maine marched triumphantly into the room, rescuing Catherine from the increasingly amused slant of the duke's smile—"I have routed Frenier and won the Battle of the Lamb! That is my good news. The bad news is that the two creatures we have the misfortune to call family are at the door and will be with us in an instant. Brace yourselves!"

9

"Aunt Honorine and Eustace, welcome, welcome." Clarendon rose to play the affable host, bringing his guests into the room. "So delighted you could come around on such short notice. I've a little surprise for you."

What an actor he'd have made, Catherine thought wryly. He looked and acted the complete family man eager to present his beloved to his loving family.

"I've invited you here today to meet the woman I've chosen to be my wife. Catherine, my dear, this is Aunt Honorine and her son, my cousin Eustace. Aunt, Eustace, this is Catherine Asterley, my betrothed."

Two pairs of small, beady eyes were riveted upon Catherine as she smiled sweetly. "It is such a great pleasure to meet Adam's family. I know the announcement is sudden, but I am sure that very soon we shall come to be friends."

For a moment neither mother nor son seemed able to speak, but stood nearly gaping at Catherine. There was no question that they were related to each other: both had the same heavy jowls, squat bodies, and blunt features. Eustace was as obese as the duke was lean, and it did not seem possible that they were relatives.

It was Aunt Honorine who recovered first. "Miss Asterley, Adam, this is quite a surprise." Her voice was shrill, an unpleasant surprise in so large a per-

son. "And, Emily, I suppose you have known of this
an age." Her tone seemed to imply the betrothal had
been deliberately kept from her.

"Hardly an age, Honorine. Only a few days." Lady
de Maine's smile did not reach her eyes, which for
once were cool. "Please be seated, won't you?" As
Honorine was taking a seat, Lady de Maine motioned Eustace to a particularly large, substantial chair
by the tea tray.

Eustace waddled to the chair. His piggy eyes, partially admiring and partially incredulous, returned to
Catherine the instant he was seated. If Catherine
could not describe his regard as murderous, neither
could she have labeled it welcoming.

"Asterley, Asterley." Honorine's beady eyes were
shrewder than her son's and held no admiring gleam
in them. "Such a sudden betrothal to a complete
stranger seems rather havey-cavey to me, Clarendon."

The duke took up his aunt's challenge in a cool,
chiding voice. "Why, Aunt Honorine, I see you are
no romantic. You would not know Catherine's family, because they were originally from Northumberland. Luckily for me, when her parents died two
years ago, she came to live with an old family friend
who is the parson in the Welsh village close to my
estate. Though her family is not of the aristocracy, I
assure you they are quite respectable; I will not be
debasing the line by my association with her."

Aunt Honorine's lips tightened, but she did not
again question Catherine's antecedents.

Catherine thought it time she played her part.
"My dear Aunt Honorine, . . . I do hope you won't
mind if I call you that?" Catherine gave the ugly face
her most enchanting smile to little, visible effect, but
she was not denied the privilege of addressing
Honorine as aunt. "I hope you will indulge us our
impetuous behavior. Clarendon, the romantic darling, quite swept me off my feet." As she spoke,

Catherine turned an adoring smile up to her employer and was rewarded with the barest hint of a twinkle.

Honorine's jowls shook when she responded with an indistinct "Hmph," while her little eyes scrutinized them carefully. It was Catherine's impression, observing the subsequent scowl that crossed Honorine's face, that the duke's aunt was both taken in by and displeased with their display of affection.

"My dear, I, for one, am delighted with your choice of a bride. Breeding tells, you know." Lady de Maine threw a superior glance at her sister-in-law before continuing. "And Catherine has the bearing of a duchess. I vow the Asterleys must have at least a baronet, if not a duke, hidden in their family tree somewhere."

Catherine nearly choked at the accuracy of the statement, while the duke, believing it to be completely inaccurate, did find it necessary to give a little cough.

Honorine, at whom the statement was aimed, gathered her wits enough to state darkly, "Time will tell." Then she turned abruptly to her nephew to ask when he planned to hold the wedding.

"As you may imagine, my dear Aunt"—he flicked a roguish glance at Catherine—"I'm eager as can be for our wedding to take place." There could be little doubt as to the meaning of his words, and Catherine felt her cheeks grow hot. "However"— his hooded eyes returned to his aunt—"Catherine believes we should wait a little to be sure we do find each other acceptable. I would say we'll hold the ceremony around Christmas or so."

"Ah, I congratulate you on your caution, Miss Asterley." Honorine bestowed a thin smile on Catherine. "So many things can come up after the ceremony that may lead one partner or the other to regret their hasty vows."

It was not much later that Honorine, apparently thinking she had learned all she could, made her farewells, her son following in her wake.

Before the front door had closed behind them, Lady de Maine rolled her eyes and gave a great whoop. "I swear that boy has become a silent pillar of flesh. He said naught beyond hello and good-bye. Indeed, he had no time, for he was too busy consuming all Chef Frenier's pastries."

"Actually he's not always so mute, especially when he's in his cups. Gad, but she is poisonous."

"So much for doing the polite to family, boy," his aunt admonished cheerfully. "Actually, I think you invited them merely to play a cat-and-mouse game with Honorine, which I must say I enjoyed."

The duke laughed, throwing a fond look at his aunt. "You are utterly incorrigible," he teased her. "And I did not invite them merely to taunt, Honorine, though I did enjoy the sport after she behaved so outlandishly."

"Thought her eyes would pop out when you first said you were betrothed! And imagine her, the wealthy but plain-as-pig's-feet daughter of a mill owner, daring to question our lovely Catherine's credentials."

"She did seem quite put out by my betrothal," the duke agreed musingly. "I wonder how much they've lived with the expectation of Eustace inheriting?"

"Can't say." Lady de Maine's shrugged. "They may not have expected you to marry. Still, you're too young for her to have counted on the title and estates coming to that half-wit anytime soon."

Catherine and the duke exchanged a glance at these words. Murder would hasten the succession, his eyes seemed to say.

The duke made his own exit soon after. "I'm to attend a mill with Freddy," he explained. "I hope you will forgive me when you realize tomorrow is

Lady Enderby's and this is my last chance for a quiet evening with my friends."

Lady de Maine responded with a dismissing snort. "Quiet evening, boy? That's doing it a bit brown, I'd say. Rousing evening is more like it."

The duke flashed his charming smile, and Catherine, observing how easily Lady de Maine succumbed to it, thought it was a very powerful weapon. "I shall give Freddy your love, Aunt Em." He chuckled. "And you, Catherine, were marvelous with Aunt Honorine and Eustace. My compliments and thanks." He raised Catherine's hand to his lips while his eyes looked directly into hers.

Catherine's hand felt very warm in his larger one. Aware of Lady de Maine's presence, Catherine left it in his grip and replied simply, "I am glad you are pleased." Then, her dimple appearing, she added, "I wish you an enjoyable evening, though I think it is too bad of you to leave me out of such sport. I have never seen a mill."

"Nor shall you, Miss Soft Heart." The duke lazily flicked her cheek with his finger. "I would be terrified lest you leap into the ring to aid the underdog."

When he had departed, the room seemed empty, though the two women sat on discussing Honorine's visit.

Infuriating or not, the Duke of Clarendon was a most powerful force, Catherine admitted with a sigh. She thought part of her attraction to the duke was the sheer novelty of masculine attention, but she was concerned where her feelings might be leading her. Remembering the thrill she had felt when he had merely taken her hand and told her how pleased he was with her acting, she made a face. It was fortunate that tomorrow night her social duties would begin, for there would be other people, and especially other attractive gentlemen, to claim some of her interest.

10

"La, Miss Catherine, but you look ever so lovely!"
Peg's dark eyes shone as she regarded her
young mistress, who looked, she enthused aloud,
"just like a princess."

Peg had arranged Catherine's shining, dark hair
on top of her head in a classic coronet. The simple,
almost severe hairstyle would not do for many women,
but on Catherine, the lack of distracting curls and
ribbons served to emphasize the perfection of her
natural beauty. Her dress, though its cut was as
classic as her hairstyle, was a sumptuous creation of
green gauze shot through with gold threads. When
Catherine moved, the golden threads caught the light,
and the dress seemed to shimmer like sunlight sparkling on water, or like the sparkle in Catherine's
amber eyes.

"You are a genius, Peg." Catherine laughed, amazed
at her transformation. "I scarcely recognize myself.
This dress and my hair put up like that make me
look like a regal stranger. I am still not certain about
this neckline, though. You really think it is not too
low?"

"Miss Catherine!" Her maid's voice held not a little
exasperation at having a subject she had thought laid
to rest raised once more. "Lady de Maine said it was
the thing, now, didn't she?"

"She told me I no longer live in the country,"
Catherine acknowledged, regarding the dress's very

à la mode neckline with a decided frown. The thick rope of pearls Lady de Maine had given her did nothing at all to help. The jewels reflected the warm pink tones of her skin and actually called attention to her swelling breasts.

Handing Catherine her long kid gloves, reticule, and fan, Peg began gently pushing her toward the door.

"It's time you went along now, Miss Catherine. They'll be waitin' on you. And you'll see, everything will be all right."

Catherine turned impulsively and gave the very startled maid a hug. "You are right to push me out the door, Peg. Left to myself, I might dive under that bed. Yes, yes, I know I must go. Wish me luck!"

When Catherine entered the blue saloon, she saw the others had already gathered. Lady de Maine sat by the fire talking to a somewhat portly gentleman with ginger-colored hair who looked to be about the duke's age. Catherine knew he must be Sir Frederick, the duke's closest friend, for he was to be their only guest.

Slowly Catherine's eyes moved to rest on the figure leaning against the mantelpiece. Her breath caught in her throat. She thought she had seen the duke looking elegant and formidable, but she had never before seen him in evening dress when his splendor could take her breath away.

Black velvet breeches and coat contrasted with a white cravat in whose intricate folds a single diamond pin gleamed. The gleam of the pin was reflected in his silver-gray eyes, which were particularly startling tonight in contrast to his dark attire. He looked to Catherine the epitome of the flawless Corinthian, and never had he seemed so beyond her touch.

A wave of anxiety assailed her when she saw he was coming to greet her. That feeling dissipated a

little when she saw his eyes widen in what looked to
be appreciation. She had passed the first and, she
admitted with a trace of chagrin, the greatest test.

"Aunt Emily's fondest wishes will be realized tonight, Catherine." The duke's white teeth flashed as
he bowed over her gloved hand. "Her chick will be
the envy of all the others present. It is a very lovely
gown."

When Catherine realized that his gaze was not, in
fact, admiring Mme Suzette's creation, but was lingering caressingly on her creamy bosom, she was
utterly powerless to prevent her hand from rising to
touch Lady de Maine's necklace.

"And Lady de Maine's gift, your grace, is it not
lovely? She has been too generous, but when I protested, she insisted, and—" Catherine's frantic tum-
ble of words were interrupted.

"It is lovely, *ma belle*." Clarendon regarded her
with an air at once amused and curious. "But it
cannot compare with you." He took hold of the hand
still clutching the necklace and gently but firmly
pulled it down. "You have no need to hide yourself,
you have nothing, absolutely nothing, to be ashamed
of. You are all that is lovely and correct."

"It is more exposure than I am accustomed to,"
Catherine admitted, searching his eyes.

"Is it?" The duke considered the concern in her
clear amber eyes and could come to no conclusion as
to its sincerity. Perhaps she did not realize that it was
acceptable for women of fashion to have a décolletage
as low as an actress might sport. "It is a style all the
ladies of the *ton* have adopted. You'll see many lower
necklines than your own."

Reassured by his words, if not that disturbing
enigmatic look, Catherine nodded.

"Though," the duke added, his silver eyes roving
downward, "I daresay that very few of them, even

with a neckline to the waist, will present such a delectable sight."

"Oh!" Catherine gasped, feeling betrayed. "Thank you very much, but I do not wish to be taken for a piece of Chef Frenier's pastry! Nor do I care to be laughed at, sir. I see you cannot appreciate my feelings, and I wish you to escort me to the others. We are neglecting them shamefully."

The duke grinned then, adding fuel to the fire. "Has anyone told you how splendidly your eyes flash when you are angry?"

Catherine's hand clenched. Her infuriating companion saw the little fist and laughed aloud. "No, no, you may not strike me. Exposing one's bosom is acceptable; striking your betrothed most assuredly is not." The duke flashed her his most appealing, boyish smile. "Forgive me, *chérie*, I confess I find myself unable to master the urge to strike a spark off you."

Was it possible, Catherine wondered as she felt her heart lurch, to resist such charm? Certainly she could not, though she did not wish him to know it.

"Pretty words, your grace. Merely pretty words. However, as I cannot afford to antagonize my leading man, I shall make a superhuman effort to forgive you."

"Then I demand a smile as proof," was the incorrigible reply.

"Oh! Have done!" Catherine wailed, the smile she had suppressed breaking through.

For a moment their gazes met and held, and Catherine experienced the unsettling sensation of being lost to all but those penetrating eyes.

Abruptly, the duke himself broke the moment with a gesture toward his friend. "Come along. As you pointed out, we are neglecting Freddy." With her hand resting lightly on his arm, he escorted her to the pair who were turning to welcome them.

"Catherine, allow me to present my oldest friend,

Sir Frederick Robertson. Freddy, wipe that school-boy look from your face and do the polite to my betrothed, Catherine Asterley."

Despite the duke's teasing words, Sir Frederick's kind brown eyes continued to admire Catherine with undaunted pleasure.

Catherine observed that Sir Frederick, though more subdued than some sprigs of fashion might be, was dressed in more colorful attire than the duke. A yellow-and-white-striped waistcoat contrasted sharply with his green satin coat, which in turn contrasted sharply with his canary-yellow knee breeches. Several rings adorned his hands while a large emerald pendant decorated his chest. Side by side the two friends were a startling contrast, one all splash and color, the other restraint and elegance. There was no doubt in Catherine's mind which man came off the best.

Sir Frederick made a low bow, acknowledging the introduction. "I am charmed, Miss Asterley. It was a stunning surprise when Adam told us the news of his betrothal. Wanted to be the first to meet the lucky girl. One look at you, though, Miss Asterley, and I see that it is Adam who is the lucky one."

Catherine's dimple appeared. "You'll put me to the blush with such kind words, Sir Frederick. I do hope we can be friends. I shall need friends to help me become accustomed to society's ways. Has Adam made clear that I am a country girl, quite unused to town?"

"If I may say so, Miss Asterley, one look at those extraordinary eyes and no man, at least, will care where you are from."

Lady de Maine greeted his words with a snort, and Freddy turned an exceedingly innocent look upon her.

"I'm only speaking the truth, Aunt Em," he said with the familiarity of a favorite friend.

"Perhaps, my boy, but Catherine is going to live among the ladies of the *ton*, too, you know."

"In any case, Miss Asterley, it will be my great pleasure to stand your friend. I hope you will call me Freddy, all my friends do."

"I would be honored to do so, Freddy. And you must call me Catherine," she replied, her amber eyes shining with delight at the pleasure of finding a friend. She had had very few in her life, and Freddy's warm brown eyes were reassuringly sincere.

Perhaps, she mused, surviving among the *beau monde* would not be as difficult as she had feared. She looked to the duke, to share her relief with him, and to her surprise saw him studying her with narrowed eyes. She was given no time to ponder the matter, however, for Davies entered to announce in sepulchral tones that dinner was served.

Dinner was a lively, informal affair during which Freddy and Lady de Maine traded the most outrageous *on-dits*, entertaining Catherine so she did not think of the duke's odd look again until they were in the hallway, and he was assisting her with her new ermine-trimmed cloak.

"A word of warning, *ma belle*," he whispered softly. "Try not to bedazzle everyone as you have Freddy. The poor man looks besotted. Remember, you are my betrothed."

Their party had moved outside, and not able to see well in the dark, Catherine was left to wonder how serious he had been. It did not seem possible that he could believe Freddy was besotted. No, she decided, it was too outrageous. The duke had surely been teasing her again.

11

"Good evening, Clarendon! So this is your intended. So lovely! We are pleased you have
brought her to our little soiree for her introduction
into society."

Lady Joanna Enderby looked, in fact, positively,
deliciously, glowingly triumphant. Which she was,
for she had succeeded in being the first hostess to
serve up the most surprising and talked about *on-dit*
of the Season. Speculation had been running ram-
pant among the members of the *ton* about the mysterious young woman who had been able to snare the
elusive and most desirable Duke of Clarendon. Now,
here she was at Lady Enderby's own soiree on the
arm of her sinfully handsome betrothed.

Catherine, aware from the corner of her eye that
Lady Enderby's booming voice had turned several
heads in their direction, felt her stomach flutter. It
suddenly seemed impossible that she could hold her
own with the sophisticates who would be present.
Lady de Maine had promised a "relative" few guests.
Two hundred people did not seem a few to Catherine, however relative.

At the threshold of the main saloon, when they
were announced, it seemed to Catherine that all four
hundred eyes turned toward them, and a hush fell
over the room. Unexpectedly, the duke gave her
hand a surreptitious squeeze. With that one gesture,
all Catherine's considerable courage returned. She

was an actress, it was merely time to exercise her craft.

Looking as assured as if she had attended glittering soirees everyday of her life, Catherine waited by the duke's side to be introduced to the scores of people hurrying to be presented to the future Duchess of Clarendon. The flawless courtesy with which the duke did so amazed Catherine. She did not know what she had expected, but the unflagging patience he exhibited, particularly in the face of the absurd simpering with which most of the ladies greeted him, was astonishing.

Although Lady de Maine had departed to observe the proceedings with the other dowagers, Freddy remained, enlivening the court she felt they were holding by whispering little asides in her ear. Never malicious, his comments were nonetheless amusing, and Catherine was often hard put to keep a decorous smile on her face. After a time, surrounded by the solicitous behavior of one escort and the amusing behavior of the other, Catherine began to relax enough to enjoy her first outing in society.

A few matrons, if they had daughters, watched Catherine's triumphant progress on the arm of their lost conquest and sniffed as if to say that, though she might be quite, quite lovely, she was still a complete unknown. But there were very few who remained disdainful after meeting her. Catherine's natural warmth, combined with her graceful, poised bearing, was difficult to resist. Soon, to her surprise, Catherine found she was a success.

The ultimate accolade was pronounced by none other than Beau Brummell, himself. "She is a diamond of the first water, Clarendon," he drawled, regarding Catherine through his quizzing glass and causing her to feel yet again like a plant specimen. "Understand you had to travel all the way to Wales to find her. An inconvenience, to be sure, but obviously worth the effort."

Catherine nearly giggled aloud at his absurd manner, but was saved from such an indiscretion by Brummell's departure and Eustace's subsequent arrival.

His jowls quivering as he tried to smile, he greeted his cousin. "Ho! Adam, Miss Asterley. Pleasure, what! Look who I've found."

As if anyone could overlook the voluptuous blond beauty by Eustace's side, thought Catherine wryly. Certainly not the duke, she was quick to note. Nor could she fail to observe how avidly his admiring regard was being returned. The beautiful woman's limpid blue eyes seemed to be drinking in the sight of Clarendon, and Catherine had the time to remark on the intimacy of that look before Eustace made the introductions.

"Catherine, allow me to present Lady Blanche Romney, wife of the Marquess of Romney. Lady Blanche, this is Catherine Asterley, the betrothed of my lucky cousin here."

The blue eyes narrowed somewhat as they made an inventory of Catherine, and only the frostiest of smiles acknowledged her. "My congratulations, Miss Asterley, you've managed to land a prime catch in a short time. It must be quite a thrill for a young, country girl."

As she considered her response, Catherine had three thoughts. First, that Eustace was not so witless as he seemed; second, that the lady's décolletage was so daring one might legitimately wonder how long she could remain decent; and third, that she would be very pleased to needle a woman to whom she had taken an instant dislike.

Smiling radiantly, Catherine did just that. "Indeed, Lady Blanche, I am very pleased and honored that Clarendon has asked me to be his wife. I feel bound to add, however, that my pleasure stems from nei- ther my youth nor my birthplace, but rather from Adam himself. I am sure you will agree he is attrac- tive enough to thrill any woman."

Blanche's responding smile was cool, but the eyes that came to rest on the duke were not. In a sud- denly husky voice she agreed. "Indeed you are at- tractive, Adam," she purred. "And I suppose I must congratulate you, too. You have certainly succeeded in turning the whole town on its ear with this very sudden betrothal of yours. What a rascal you can be!" Lady Blanche playfully tapped the duke's arm with her fan and allowed the tiniest hint of a pout to be suggested on her red lips. "But I beseech you to promise that you will not allow any new acquaint- ances to come between old friends."

Clarendon, looking faintly amused, bowed. "Blanche, you look lovely, as always." His tone of voice sounded seductive to Catherine's sensitive ear. "But I must correct the impression you seem to have. Cath- erine, although an acquaintance, will be much more than that as my wife. Still," he paused a moment before adding enigmatically, "I am sure I shan't for- get old friends just because I am wed."

Something for everyone and not enough for any- one, Catherine thought nastily. She wondered just how friendly the old friends were.

"I hope not, my dear." Lady Blanche smiled archly. "In fact, I was hoping your intended, Miss, er, Asterley, would excuse you a moment. I've a matter I simply must discuss privately with you."

The duke clearly hesitated, and Catherine, though she chided herself for her reaction, felt stung by his hesitation. Before he could speak, she rushed to say, "Why, Adam, how ungallant you are to hesitate over such a pretty plea. I shall do famously with Freddy and Eustace to entertain me. Do go on, it will give me an opportunity to spread my wings a bit."

Surprise flashed in Lady Blanche's eyes, while the duke's expression remained impassive. Only an imperceptible narrowing of his eyes indicated he was not entirely pleased with Catherine's cordial words.

When the duke and Lady Blanche had departed, Catherine dispatched Eustace by politely asking if he would obtain a glass of lemonade punch for her. As soon as she was alone with Freddy, she turned her steady amber gaze upon him.

"Whoever is that catty woman, Freddy?"

"Hmph," that gentleman snorted, feeling he'd been left to handle a rather touchy issue without any direction. "Lady Blanche is the wife of the Marquess of Romney."

When he said nothing more, Catherine felt it necessary to encourage him. "And how does she know Adam?"

"Oh, Adam, er, well, before she married, before he went to the Peninsula, ages ago you know, they were, er, quite close."

"Did they have an affair, Freddy?"

Freddy winced at the bold question. "Catherine, really, it's not good form to ask such questions!"

Freddy, who had been dreading an angry scene, was touched to see a fleeting, wistful look appear in his companion's eyes. Surprising himself, he rushed to reassure her. "Whatever was between them is in the past, Catherine. I assure you, the Adam I know is too honorable to speak false words of affection."

"You are not to worry, Freddy." Catherine gave him a gallant little smile that quite undid him. "I know Adam's feelings quite well, and I have no doubts regarding his intentions."

Out of the corner of her eye, she could see the duke's dark head bending toward Lady Blanche's blond one. Before she looked away, Catherine saw a slow, intimate smile curve his slightly mocking lips. It was a sight that caused her pain, she was sorry to realize. She thought it likely, from what Freddy had said, that Lady Blanche was the woman referred to in the servants' gossip. The duke had once loved her, and though she had married another, it was obvious to Catherine that Lady Blanche still held his interest.

"I say, Freddy, good to see you this evening." The words were spoken in hearty tones by a young dandy whom Freddy introduced as Lord Quinsey. Lord Quinsey turned with telling speed to admire Catherine's delightful smile, but had her to himself for only a moment when another young gentleman neatly elbowed him aside. Just as quickly, the second gentleman suffered the same fate as had Lord Quinsey. All those young men who had been too daunted to seek the acquaintance of Clarendon's beautiful betrothed while he stood guard by her side, took advantage of his absence to besiege the much-less-formidable Freddy, and Catherine soon became the center of a large, admiring group.

Catherine, who had never had the opportunity to enjoy such polite and harmless attention, found it a very pleasant antidote to the dismal feelings aroused by the sight of Lady Blanche and the duke. Her eyes sparkled as she responded playfully to the young gentlemen surrounding her.

The duke, by lifting his eyes a fraction above Lady Blanche's golden coiffure, was able to observe his supposed bride-to-be apparently delighting in the adoring attention of half the men in the room. Had he been honest, he might also have noted there were a few women in the group surrounding her, but he was not in the mood to be so honest. She looked to him like an actress in the green room choosing her next provider.

Blanche regained his attention by leaning into his arm and whispering in his ear. A lazy smile re-

warded her efforts until a gay laugh floated across
the room. As the duke heard it, his head jerked up.
He was not pleased to see that Freddy had introduced Catherine to Lord Charles Musgrave. Lord
Musgrave was a handsome, sophisticated man whom
the duke had know since their schooldays. They had
over the years shared many experiences, and the
duke was well aware that Charles Musgrave's serious
demeanor was most attractive to a great many women,
as was his adequate income. As he watched, Charles
raised Catherine's slender hand to his lips, and a
pleased-looking smile curved Catherine's generous
mouth in response.

It happened that Clarendon was not entirely amiss
in his assessment of the situation, for Catherine did
think Lord Charles Musgrave's blond good looks
and clear-blue eyes most attractive. She also found
his company more enjoyable than that of the other,
younger men who had thronged about her. Like
puppies, they were entertaining and often appealing, but, alas, essentially mindless. Lord Musgrave,
though more sedate, had, she found after the initial
pleasantries, something of interest to say. With a
twinkle in his eye he told her that in spite of his
elegant exterior he was a farmer at heart.

"Now, you will not start on the importance of crop
rotation, Charles," Freddy admonished, looking mortified at the possibility of so utterly plebeian a topic
being raised. "It will bore Catherine to death."

But he did not, yet, know Catherine very well.
"Indeed, a discussion of crop rotation will not bore
me, Freddy," she corrected his error with a playful
smile. "Remember, I am from the country and know
a bit on the subject myself."

Thus encouraged, Lord Musgrave launched into a
dissertation on the latest farming methods to which
Catherine listened with interest. However, when

Charles began to reply to one of Catherine's interested questions, Freddy could stand no more.

"Spare me! I beg you. Catherine may be unbelievably interested in all this talk of planting, but I am bored to tears."

"But shame on you, Freddy, you ought to take an interest in farming," Catherine chided, her eyes dancing at the thought of Freddy's sartorial splendor anywhere near a field. "Your land depends on good management, as you must know."

"That is precisely why I hire a manager, Catherine," he responded, rolling his eyes. "Couldn't grow a weed if I tried."

When Catherine laughingly agreed to relent, Lord Musgrave turned to her. "You are a rare woman, Miss Asterley. Beauty is not often so interesting. I think it's quite unfair of you to attach yourself to Adam before giving the rest of us a chance. You must let me tell you all of his history. Perhaps once you've got an idea what a rum thing he is, you might change your mind."

"I hope you don't propose to bore us with old history, Musgrave," the man in question drawled from behind them.

Catherine, a sparkling smile in her eyes, turned to greet him, but her welcoming words died unsaid. An icy chill in his gray eyes froze her welcome and sent a frisson of alarm through her.

"Adam!" Charles appeared impervious to his friend's coolness. "You dog, with your usual luck, you've found a rare gem. I congratulate you on having the good sense to claim her. And I trust you will allow me the honor of taking her for a ride in my phaeton tomorrow."

No answering smile softened the duke's hawklike face, but after the briefest pause he inclined his head a fraction to signify his agreement.

"Well, I cannot allow Charles to steal a march on

me," Freddy declared in an aggrieved voice. "Do you ride, Catherine?"

Catherine, deliberately disregarding her employer's coolness, laughed aloud at the question. Over half her childhood had been spent on Lightning. "I adore riding, Freddy, but I have not been able to ride since I left the country." And feared never to ride again, she added to herself.

In her eagerness Catherine agreed to ride with Freddy before the duke's permission had been obtained. Seeing Freddy's quick, anxious glance, Catherine hurried to repair the omission. "That is, I accept with your permission, of course, Adam."

She dared another look at her employer. He was still angry, perhaps angrier, and hesitating to permit her to ride with Freddy, it seemed, as he continued to be silent.

"Perhaps you'd care to join us?" Freddy asked, a trifle awkwardly.

"Not at all," was the unequivocal reply, "Three would be *de trop.* Of course, by all means, accompany Freddy, Catherine. I should hate to put a damper on anything you would adore doing."

"Thank you." Catherine's voice was as curt as his was mocking, for her temper was rising in response to his inexplicably unpleasant mood. Rebelliously she vowed to enjoy the rest of the evening despite him, though in truth she was not able to give Lady Enderby's singers the attention they deserved. Seated by the duke's side, she was not able to ignore his icy silence and could only wonder uneasily about its cause.

12

The carriage ride home was worse. Lady de Maine could not stop exclaiming over Catherine's success, being particularly pleased that Sally Jersey had commended her for turning out such a perfect gem, but hers were the only high spirits in the group. Catherine, glancing at the duke's shuttered face, could feel her stomach knot. With a feeling of dread she recalled thinking the first time she met him that she would not care to be his enemy, and now inexplicably she was. Escape to the relative safety of her room could not come too soon.

Escape did not prove possible, however. When they arrived at Clarendon House, the duke informed her tightly that he wished to see her in his study. Lady de Maine protested that it was too late for a talk, but Clarendon informed his aunt in a tone that brooked no opposition that the matter had best be seen to now. He considered Lady de Maine's feelings only enough to add that he would not keep Catherine long.

Trailing after him to his study, Catherine felt very like a schoolboy called before the master. When she closed the door, she kept her back against it and herself as far as possible from the man leaning against his desk, his arms crossed over his broad chest.

"Sit!" The crack of the word made Catherine jump, and though she wanted to remain standing, as he was, she had the distinct feeling she should take a seat. His glare never left her as she walked, her back stiff, to her seat. Once seated, she clasped together hands that seemed suddenly very cold, composing herself for whatever was to follow. She had not long to wait. His voice sliced the air, the contempt in it so great her cheeks first colored, then paled.

"Your performance tonight was disgusting. I will not stand for it again. The brazen manner you displayed belongs in the theater, not a polite drawing room."

"Brazen!" Catherine gaped at him. The sweeping denouncement stunned her for a moment. But his eyes never wavered, and seeing that he meant what he said, she was galvanized by righteous anger. "How dare you imply such an odious thing!" she blazed back. "My behavior was approved by everyone present, witness your own aunt in the carriage, or Brummell, or Lady Jersey, or, or Freddy. How else could I act the part of a betrothed girl meeting the friends of her intended?"

Clarendon's lip curled with disdain. He uncoiled from his desk to loom over her, looking enormous, but Catherine refused to shrink from him.

"It won't wash, you little strumpet," he ground out. "The smiles and simperings you bestowed on half a dozen men—Charles Musgrave in particular— were scarcely those of a betrothed woman simply out to meet a few friends. They were meant to secure attention and did so quite successfully. I shall remind you this once that you are being paid—and handsomely, I might add—to act the part of an adoring bride, not to collect a wealthy husband."

When Catherine gasped and would have denied his words, he roared, "Silence! My aunt and all the rest have accepted you as a respectable girl of good family, but we both know you are not a sweet, young thing, don't we? You are nothing but an actress with the same lack of morals enjoyed by everyone in your

profession. You miscalculated badly if you thought
I'd not notice when you demonstrated your considerable skills with my sex tonight. Be warned, Catherine, that I will never allow you to use the background
I have created to hoodwink a respectable member of
society into matrimony."

The hurtful words assaulted her, freezing her with
such horror she was unable to respond. She had
been idiot enough to think he had begun to revise
his opinion of actresses, or at least of her. She thought
they had become friends—nothing more, of course—
but still friends joined in a partnership. Now she saw
it had all been pretense; he had only been playing
his role and she had deceived herself. A loud oath
scattered her thoughts.

The duke was directly before her, his face a mask
of fury, and before she had time to resist, he jerked
her to her feet. Shaking her as if she were a rag doll,
he growled fiercely, "Do you think you can escape
me by turning a deaf ear?"

Catherine's hair tumbled from its pins and flew
wildly about her shoulders. "Stop!" she cried, raising
her fists despite the painful hold he had on her arms
to strike at his chest.

"So the little cat has claws." The duke caught her
arms behind her back with one large hand, pinning
her body to his. She could feel how hard his muscles
were, though she was more acutely aware of the
awful power of his steely eyes.

"Perhaps you did not care if I noticed you tonight.
Perhaps you thought you could secure my conniv-
ance in your scheme." No longer harsh, the duke's
voice was soft as velvet, but it held such menace that
Catherine shuddered involuntarily. She felt truly
afraid for the first time.

"Let me go," she begged.

"Did you think to win my silence with your charms,

Catherine?" he asked, paying no heed. "When was I to be given my taste?"

Catherine watched, trapped in his hold, as his glittering silver eyes dropped to her mouth.

"No," she cried, twisting her head frantically.

"Oh, yes," he insisted, his mouth descending to hers.

Catherine had never been kissed on the mouth by anyone before. She had dreamed of it, of course, as every girl does. Not one of her dreams had been remotely like this. Her soft lips felt bruised by the intent, plundering mouth taking hers so ruthlessly. A strangled cry escaped her when his teeth scraped her soft lip.

At the sound, the duke pulled back suddenly and with a vicious curse released her so abruptly she fell backward into her chair. Her heart was pounding as if she had run for miles, and she could feel tears, wet and cold, on her cheeks. She had no thought to flee; she felt too dazed to form a coherent thought.

The duke still stood above her, glaring at her bowed head. He took in her disheveled hair, spread like a silky curtain around her, her pale cheeks, her hands clenched tightly in her lap, and finally the blood on her lip. The blazing fury in his eyes cooled abruptly.

He withdrew a white handkerchief from his pocket, and, flinging it to her, watched while she dabbed her lip. If his hand reached out momentarily as if he would attend to the matter himself, Catherine did not see it, and the derisive voice with which he addressed her next indicated no softening of his attitude.

"Let that be a lesson to you, Miss Wright. I will not tolerate being used. In the future you will avoid private engagements with any man. You will not accept any invitation unless it includes me or Aunt Emily."

He paused, contempt for her turning his eyes to a

slate gray. Her continued silence seemed to goad him, and he added in a taut voice that lashed her, "I promise you, Catherine, that what you have seen tonight will be nothing compared to the punishment you will receive if I find you have not heeded me. Do I make myself clear?"

Catherine sat, her head still bowed, clenching Clarendon's bloodstained handkerchief. She longed to toss it and any further contact with him in his hateful face. It was unbearable to think she must continue to associate with him, knowing how vilely he thought of her.

Yet, she wondered, suddenly feeling very tired, what else was she to do? She had no funds and she had nowhere to go to earn them. Mr. Trevinian would not hire her back until Mme Rosa had left, and that was not likely to be for a year or more. She could return to Northumberland, but even the duke's painful accusations were preferable to Rudolph's ruthless, greedy clutches. The bitter angry words on her tongue died. It seemed she could not even afford her pride.

In a small, tight voice she surrendered. "I accept your condition, your grace," she said. Then, pulling the last shreds of her battered dignity about her, Catherine rose. She put the chair between them, a fact the duke did not miss, and raised her pale face to address him with a level, determined look. "However, I also have a condition, your grace. No one has ever treated me as you have done tonight. If you ever lay your hands upon me again, I shall leave your employ. Whatever you may think of me, I do not deserve such abusive treatment, and I will not accept it."

Very few people had ever dared to set a condition upon the Duke of Clarendon, and he was compelled, almost against his will, to admire the bravery of the minx eyeing him so resolutely. Her lip might be trembling, but her chin was up and her spine was rigid.

"If you act as you should, then I shall," the duke's voice was curt. "But I will not answer for my behavior if you provoke me again."

"Then, we are each forewarned, your grace." Catherine's tone challenged, though she had to struggle to hold back tears. But she would not, she insisted fiercely, she would absolutely not cry before him. "Is that all?"

At the duke's nod, she forced herself to walk, not run, from the room, intensely aware all the while of his eyes boring into her back.

Catherine cried that night for the first time since her mother's death. After Peg had been dismissed, after she had lain hollow-eyed in her bed for an hour, when the duke's contemptuous words began to ring one by one in her ears, great sobs welled up from deep within her. Long into the night she cried for her wounded pride, for her helplessness, and finally, for the flimsy dreams of a silly girl.

13

"For the life of me, I cannot understand why Honorine has been so prompt with an invitation to visit, and I find it curious she made no mention of it last night at the Enderbys'. Now she's sent it around this morning, addressed to you. But she won't avoid me that easily, child. I shan't let you face the dragon alone."

"Are you to be my Saint George, then, dear lady?" Catherine smiled at Lady de Maine's grimace.

"Well, I may not slay her, but I shall certainly see she doesn't slay you."

Lady de Maine's words caused Catherine to give her a sharp look and then to chide herself for an overactive imagination. Whatever the purpose of Honorine's invitation—and that was a puzzle—it would scarcely be to serve poisoned tea.

Returning her thoughts to her hostess, she heard Lady de Maine saying, "Besides, after our visit to Honorine, I thought we might visit Bond Street. There are the other pelisses to purchase, and perhaps some slippers for—"

"Slippers! That's a new one!" Catherine grinned. "I would remind you I've half a dozen pairs, but I know there is little use persisting in my efforts to make you see any sense in the matter of my wardrobe. However, I really cannot go today, for I am engaged to go for a ride in the park with Lord Charles Musgrave this afternoon. Perhaps we could resume our shopping spree tomorrow, after my morning ride with Freddy."

"What is this?" Lady de Maine exclaimed, her eyes alight with satisfaction. "You didn't tell me last night, you naughty girl. Two gentlemen already beating a path to your door. How perfectly delightful!"

How perfectly differently the duke had seen the same situation, Catherine thought bitterly. She had awakened that morning heavy-eyed and unable for a moment to think why she should feel so. Then, like a specter, the duke's scornful face had risen in her mind. Was it possible, she had asked herself, that his words, if not his actions, had merit? Remembering how she had gone unescorted with him to the inn in Bath, Catherine worried that her isolation as a child, followed by her association with the theater, had left her without a reasonable feeling for proper conduct.

Reviewing the evening as dispassionately as possible, however, she noted that she had been a success with the older matrons as well as the younger men, and that Lady de Maine, who was quite as haughty in her way as the duke was in his, had approved of her manner. No, Clarendon, unable to believe anyone associated with the theater was not depraved, had seen what he wanted to see.

Her mind turned to the kiss he had forced upon her. In all her girlish thoughts on the subject, she had never imagined such a simple act could be laden with such feeling. But what dreadful feelings! She clenched her fist at the thought that her first kiss had been administered as a punishment. If only she had had the presence of mind to slap his offending mouth ... It galled her today to recall how meekly she had sat before him with her head bowed. Oh! she did not wish to see the Duke of Clarendon for a good while.

Avoiding him turned out to be an easy matter, for only Lady de Maine was present at the breakfast table, holding Honorine's invitation in her hand, a perplexed look on her face. Catherine was as mystified as Lady de Maine by Honorine's intentions, but she declared immediately that she would go. Though she was not particularly eager to visit Honorine, Catherine was glad to have something to distract her.

A short while later the two ladies arrived at a town house on the edge of the fashionable Mayfair district. The house was large and obviously costly, but the address was not the very best, certainly not as impressive as the duke's address in Berkeley Square. Catherine wondered how much Honorine might resent the discrepancy.

They found Honorine in the "Egyptian room," her vast bulk ensconced in a chair whose sturdy legs were carved to resemble palm trees. Catherine, as she sat uncomfortably on a backless couch, observed with interest how Honorine's smile never quite reached her shrewd little eyes.

"I cannot say I cared for Madame Veracci's voice," Honorine lamented when the housekeeper had left them with the tea tray. "But so few really gifted singers are willing to sing at private gatherings anymore. They say it strains their voices and leaves them too tired to perform well at the Opera House."

Lady de Maine delivered a few words in support of the singer, and Honorine turned to Catherine. "What do you think, Miss Asterley? Oh, but perhaps you were too distracted to really listen to Madame Veracci at all?"

At Catherine's look of polite inquiry Honorine continued smoothly, her reptillian eyes unwavering. "You were so calm in the face of Lady Blanche's attentions to Adam, but I cannot imagine you did not notice them. I do not want to interfere in your affairs, my dear, but as you said, we are your family now and I think it is my duty to warn you about that situation."

Though Catherine was not entirely surprised by Honorine's attack, it had been swift, and she felt her cheeks color. Apparently satisfied that she had scored a hit, Honorine added in a confiding tone, "Perhaps you are not aware that Lady Blanche and Adam were very much in love at one time, Catherine. Feelings of that depth are hard to forget, I am afraid."

Lady de Maine looked as if she might respond, but Honorine swept on. "Such a shock our poor Adam sustained when she wouldn't have him. We all expected their betrothal as a matter of course, but instead of Adam, Blanche chose a title and money. Of course, Marchioness of Romney is nothing compared to Duchess of Clarendon, but how was she to know the younger son would succeed?"

Lady de Maine, having at last gathered her wits about her, broke in, her eyes sparkling with outrage. "Most men, Honorine, have early infatuations, but I am quite certain that Adam's warm feelings toward Blanche Romney were irrevocably changed by her capricious behavior."

"Perhaps, perhaps, Emily," replied Honorine smugly. "However, he did hie off to the Peninsula campaign, and they say he was quite reckless in his exploits there. How else may we explain such behavior, except as due to a broken heart?"

"In the first place, waiting five years to go is scarcely hieing off! And in the second, his behavior was never reckless. He was only being extremely brave, as Wellington wrote in his dispatches. Adam always wanted to take part in the campaign against that rascal Bonaparte, and he did his part honorably, not like a good many idle wastrels I could name."

Honorine's chins were set to quivering by the thinly veiled reference to Eustace, but she was not disconcerted for long. She had some powerful ammunition to use, and Catherine judged from the look in her eye that Honorine was more than a little pleased to use it.

"Whatever you may say about his military exploits, Emily, you cannot deny that there has been talk of Adam and Blanche since his return. That is one reason everyone has been so surprised by his betrothal to Catherine."

"I should hope you would have better things to do than to repeat gossip, Honorine," Lady de Maine snapped. "I know that Adam would never undertake matrimony with Catherine if his feelings were still engaged by Blanche."

Until now Catherine had only listened, curious as to what Honorine might say. It surprised her that Honorine would attempt to separate the betrothed pair so openly, but she reflected that Honorine did not seem to be a particularly subtle person. Coldly Catherine put all thought of the duke and his lady love aside. It mattered not one whit to her that her surmises about their relationship had been correct. The catty blonde was welcome to him.

When Lady de Maine fell silent, Catherine made a little gesture to bring all eyes to her. "Dear me." Her amber eyes opened innocently. "I never thought old friends could create such a stir. For my part I am very pleased with Ad, er, Clarendon's attentions. Indeed, last night he invited me to the study when we returned home. I know you thought it late, Aunt Emily, but it was an important matter, at least to us. He told me then that he had been quite pleased with my success at the Enderbys', and said he could see no reason why we should not hold our wedding much sooner than December. He is so impatient, he is insisting we marry this summer. He does particularly desire to start a nursery."

The thwarted look that crossed Honorine's heavy face nearly made Catherine laugh aloud, and when she joined Lady de Maine in the carriage after their polite but somewhat strained good-byes, she felt better than at any time since her visit to the duke's study.

In the carriage Lady de Maine fell back into the squabs giving a very un-Lady de Maine-like screech. "What an awful woman! I must apologize for our family, Catherine. However Rupert could have married such a vile person is, and always has always been, utterly beyond me." Her face creased with concern, she turned to Catherine. "My dear, it is my very sincere belief that Adam is too fine a man to deceive you. He would not do such a thing, I am sure of it." Lady de Maine's tone was adamant, though her eyes fell away from Catherine's.

Catherine ignored the evasiveness, smiling instead. "Dear Aunt Em, I pray you, do not let Honorine upset you. Everything will be well, you'll see. How could it not be with a champion like you by my side? You were marvelous with Honorine. I thought you might run her through at any minute!"

Lady de Maine gave a little laugh, but her expression remained earnest. "My dear, I won't deceive you. While I never cared for Blanche Elliott, Adam did. He was young and she was the acclaimed beauty of her Season. She enjoyed the attentions of all the young bucks, but particularly our handsome, dashing Adam. However, she never intended marriage, only dangling him and all the others on a string until she received an offer that would provide her both wealth and a title, regardless of her feelings for the person making the offer. The Marquess of Romney is twenty-five years Blanche's senior and is as unprepossessing as is possible. I admit, I, too, have heard rumors since Adam's return from the Peninsula, but, Catherine, I know him to be an honorable man and I cannot believe he will be anything but a good husband and father."

Catherine was deeply touched by Lady de Maine's concern for her nephew and for her, and silently cursed Honorine. Taking both the older woman's hands in hers, Catherine smiled. "I do not care what the rumors are. I am very certain of how Adam feels about me, Aunt Em. You must not worry about us one moment longer, for you only give Honorine a victory in that case. She is a mischief-maker, and you simply must not listen to her nonsense. I promise you, I shall not."

"Oh, my love, you are such a dear, and you are in the right of it. It is only Honorine's mischief. I cannot think why she is being so vicious. Imagine, inviting you to her home to fill you full of doubts. But look! You are too wise for her and you have not let her upset you in the least. Instead, you are left to attend to me, fool that I am."

Catherine blushed, turning away from Lady de Maine's trusting face to look out the window. How very uncomfortable it was to be able to convince some people to believe lies, while others she could not convince to believe the truth. Perhaps living with the duke's distrust was meant to be her penance for so misleading his aunt, though she was not certain even that could absolve her.

Once home, Davies informed the ladies that his grace had sent word he would be absent for luncheon, giving Catherine another reprieve. With any luck, she thought she could avoid his grace the entire day. Tomorrow would be soon enough to inform him of his ardent desire to hasten their nuptials. What a fabrication that was. If the truth were known, the duke would sooner allow Eustace to remain his heir than marry the likes of her.

"Catherine!" Lady de Maine's voice, brimming with excitement, interrupted her grim thoughts. "Just imagine what you have received. Vouchers for Almack's! And so soon! Sally Jersey sent them 'round. She was much taken with you last evening, but I am surprised she acted so promptly. Oh, I am so delighted. It washes the taste of Honorine out of my mouth."

Catherine smiled, a genuine smile of pleasure. The coveted vouchers were another proof that her disparaging employer stood quite alone in his opinion of her.

14

*C*atherine, dressed in a stylish blue afternoon dress trimmed with Mechlin lace and wearing a fetching straw bonnet, stood before Lord Charles Musgrave's high-perch phaeton later that day eyeing it with obvious apprehension.

"It may look fragile, Miss Asterley, but on my honor, I have come to no harm yet, and I have owned it for several weeks."

Catherine smiled into her escort's twinkling blue eyes. "I confess your gleaming conveyance seems a mere toy to me, Sir Charles. It is astonishingly high, is it not?"

"It is a very high phaeton, in fact. but it is also a marvel of design and is quite well-balanced. That is not to say some young pup with little experience would find it an easy drive, but I assure you I have enough experience to bring you home safely."

"Of course you have, my lord, and I am ashamed to have entertained the smallest doubt." Catherine's dimple peeped out. "Am I forgiven?"

"There is nothing to forgive so charming a lady, especially as this is her first ride in such a conveyance."

"Ah! You are making allowances for my country ways, I see."

His lordship smiled into the sparkling amber eyes of his companion. "Perhaps, though I rather doubt I would be so accommodating for a country dowd."

"And charming, too. But"—Catherine turned back

to the rather absurd vehicle—"how do I scale your phaeton?"

Lord Musgrave laughed outright at Catherine's puzzled look and proceeded to show her how, with his assistance, she could easily take her seat.

After he was seated and his groom mounted behind them, they set off, quite safely, it seemed, for the park.

"I am surprised Adam hasn't taken you out," Musgrave said. "I must own he is the superior whip. In our youth he won all the races, even setting a still-unbroken record for the Bath stage."

"And do you race now, Sir Charles?" Catherine asked, wishing to discuss any subject other than that of her supposed husband-to-be.

Lord Musgrave replied that, though he no longer raced, he was interested in racing and, with a question or two from Catherine, was off on a long discussion of the finer points of a good racehorse.

As he talked, Catherine noticed that Sir Charles' coat of blue superfine covered shoulders almost as broad as the duke's, and that his blue eyes were filled with kindness rather than mockery. His blond hair curled around a face that, if it was not quite so handsome as her employer's, was a good deal more open. There would be little trouble reading his emotions, Catherine thought with a little sigh. Nor, for all his sophistication, did she think the emotions reflected on Sir Charles' face would be terribly complex. He seemed to be exactly what he had said: a man who preferred the simpler pursuits of the country. It took little effort for Catherine to imagine him living in quiet, rustic content with a sweet, kind wife and a band of equally sweet, well-behaved children.

Biting her lip, Catherine angrily mocked herself for comparing Sir Charles to her employer. His shoulders were narrower, his intellect less lofty, his manner less challenging—and his temper much sweeter.

Yet, she realized uneasily, whatever the final tally, Lord Charles Musgrave stirred no interest in her breast. Not, of course, that it would have mattered if he had, for, as she had been so rudely reminded the night before, he was utterly beyond her aspirations. Still, for one reason or another, it was disquieting to find herself so uninterested in such a fine specimen of manhood.

Within a short while, they reached the park, and Catherine put aside her wayward thoughts when she caught sight of the crush of people there.

"Everyone comes to see everyone" was Sir Charles' reply to her exclamation. Everyone included many of the same people she had met at Lady Enderby's. Lady Jersey stopped to chat, allowing Catherine to thank her for the vouchers to Almack's, and Brummell again singled her out, going so far as to call her "the most refreshing new light on the social scene."

Lord Musgrave had gone only a little distance farther, when another phaeton, a somewhat older one, pulled up beside them.

"Lynsford, Lady Anne." Musgrave's voice was cool as he acknowledged the man, but warmed considerably when he addressed the young woman. Catherine looked curiously at the girl who inspired his interest.

To her surprise Catherine saw rather plain, sandy-brown hair and a sweet, though certainly not beautiful face. Ah, but the eyes of the young woman, introduced as Lady Anne Lynsford, were quite fine, Catherine realized. Large, of hazel color, they were turned with a luminous appreciation upon Sir Charles. Evidently the interest Sir Charles felt was returned.

Turning to gauge the other man's reaction, Catherine caught him staring at her, not the others. In the moment before a smile of welcome crossed his face, the man introduced as the Marquess of Lynsford had been scrutinizing her with narrowed pale-blue eyes, his surprising expression reminding Catherine of a fox. In the very next instant, however, the intent look vanished and the marquess smiled cordially.

"It is a pleasure to meet so lovely a lady, Miss Asterley. I understand now why Clarendon has abruptly decided to undertake marriage, a state he has resisted so adamantly until now. Your beauty could change even the most hardened bachelor's mind."

The words were unexceptionable, but for some reason they did little to thaw Catherine. There was some indefinable air about the Marquess of Lynsford that repelled her. Subduing any outward sign of her feelings, she responded politely, thanking him for his kind words. As soon as possible, however, she turned to his sister with a greeting.

A few moments later, having been an obstacle to the flow of traffic for long enough, the two couples nodded their farewells and the phaetons pulled part.

Catherine did not miss the fervent look Lady Anne cast Sir Charles' way after her brother had turned his head, and could not forbear to comment. "Such lovely eyes Lady Anne has."

"Yes, I suppose so." Musgrave's voice was stiff.

Catherine glanced up, grinning at his determinedly disinterested response.

Sir Charles saw her expression, and his own relaxed into a rueful smile. "Am I that obvious?"

"Actually not," Catherine assured him. "I got the first inkling from your greeting, but it was only when I saw Lady Anne's eyes widen with happiness that I really suspected."

Catherine saw a brief spark of pleasure light Sir Charles' eyes, but it was quenched almost immediately by a dark frown.

"Whatever is the matter?" asked Catherine with concern.

"It's her wretched brother." The words seemed to burst from him as if he had no control over them. With a groan, Sir Charles raked his hand through his hair, his expression the picture of distraction. "I shouldn't tell you any of this, we have agreed to tell no one of our feelings, but I cannot bear the silence a moment longer. Do you care to listen to a lover's lament, Miss Asterley?"

Catherine nodded, observing now the lines of care hidden by Lord Musgrave's normally smiling expression. He looked out over the heads of his horses, his expression quite serious. "I met Anne last Season at some rout or other, and I liked her immediately. She was so unlike the other young girls, who seem to be interested only in themselves or what title a prospective suitor does or does not have. Anne is thoughtful, warm, and intelligent. She is what I want for my wife: someone I can make a meaningful life with, someone who loves the country as I do and would not resent being out of the social whirl. To my delight she returned my feelings, but when I went to ask Lynsford for her hand, he refused me."

"Good heavens, why?" Catherine could imagine no one most brothers would rather have pay suit to their sisters than the kind, handsome man seated next to her.

"Money," was the bitter reply.

At Catherine's look of complete astonishment, Charles shrugged. "Oh, I have enough to be comfortable. Enough for Anne's tastes, but I've not enough for Lynsford. His father left him almost a pauper, and Lynsford has done little to save what he had. Has very grand ideas, does our Marquess of Lynsford. Consequently he needs a brother-in-law who will settle an enormous portion on him and be prepared to support his grandiose style for life. In short, someone far wealthier than Lord Charles Musgrave, I'm afraid."

"But that is horrid! To deny his sister's perfectly reasonable wishes for his own selfish ends." Having been in something of the same situation, Catherine felt an instant sympathy for the pair of lovers.

"I'm afraid he has every right to arrange Anne's affairs as he sees fit." Charles could not keep the anger from his voice. "However horrid his wishes may be, he is her guardian."

"But what shall you do? You cannot mean to accept such outrageous behavior?"

"What can we do, Miss Asterley? If we elope, society will condemn us. I do not believe I can ask Anne to live such a life simply for my sake. We live with it the best we can, meeting in secret, if it can be arranged, or snatching a few words here and there when Lynsford's back is turned. My only hope is that Lynsford will not find a better suitor. If he does not, he will be forced to accept me."

"Well, I shall do anything in my limited power to aid you, Sir Charles. You have only to ask."

They had in the course of their conversation arrived once more at Clarendon House, and Charles pulled his horses to a halt.

"Thank you, Miss Asterley. I should never have burdened you with my problems, but I feel sometimes I might go mad without anyone to talk to. Thank you for listening. You are as kind as you are beautiful, which is rare, you know. Adam is indeed a lucky man." He saluted Catherine's hand with a kiss.

Touched by the kind words, Catherine gave his large hand a squeeze in return and smiled warmly. "And I can understand what inspired such a loving look in Lady Anne's lovely eyes, Sir Charles. Please believe me when I say I wish to help."

"You won't say anything about this to anyone, even Adam? He's closemouthed, but things have a way of getting about the more people know of them. The secrecy is not for me, but for Anne. She believes Lynsford would be incensed if he thought we were trying to turn public opinion against him. Apparently he has a nasty temper and might forbid the match for that reason alone."

Catherine patted the hand still holding hers and assured him she would honor his request.

"I see you enjoyed your drive," a familiar, cool voice drawled.

Catherine spun about to see the duke standing on the steps of the house, observing them with hooded eyes. A slow, burning flush crept up her cheeks as she realized the interpretation that he would likely put on the scene. She forced herself not to jerk her hand from Charles' grasp.

"Adam, I was just telling Miss Asterley . . ." Charles began, trying to pull his own thoughts back to the present.

"Yes, I could gather the tenor of your words from the look on your face. No need to go into detail, my boy."

At any other time even Charles might have noted the duke's brusque manner, but not today. He was too distracted by his own dilemma to pay attention to anyone else.

"Shall we see you at White's this evening, Adam?" he asked.

"No, I've other plans for the evening," the duke replied indifferently. He had reached the phaeton, and Catherine realized he had come to help her down as any doting betrothed might do.

He ignored her outstretched hand, placing his hands around her slender waist instead. To keep from falling forward, Catherine was forced to place her hands on his shoulders, bringing her face close to his. Her eyes dwelt for a moment on his mouth, remembering with a stab of anguish the bruising feel of it. From there her gaze was irresistibly drawn to his. It was a temptation she should have resisted, for his eyes held not a flicker of warmth.

Immediately, Catherine tried to free herself from

his hold, but his grip on her waist only tightened. While one hand waved Charles farewell, the other held Catherine by his side.

"Such a pretty picture you made perched on Charles' phaeton, Catherine," the duke mocked her when Lord Charles had gone. "I trust, however, it is the last time I shall be treated to it."

Catherine's eyes blazed hotly at the undeserved insult. "It was an innocent scene, your grace. Only your jaded eyes have corrupted it," she flung at him. "I am amazed you believe your friend, a man of the world with a great deal of experience with women, would be so foolish as to be ensnared by me."

Slowly, retaining his grip, the duke leaned back, his hooded eyes falling to Catherine's soft lips. A sardonic smile twisted his mouth, and his eyes moved to her breasts. After lingering on them a moment, his gaze traveled down to her slim waist and then dropped to her rounded hips. The inventory completed, his cool eyes returned to flick her flushed face. "In fact, my dear, I think Charles is a most discriminating man."

With those cryptic words the duke bowed and strode to his carriage, leaving Catherine to look after him, the angry heat still stinging her cheeks.

15

Catherine bid the young footman good morning, her smile inviting him to share her pleasure at the beauty of the day. Her spirits were high this morning, for she was anticipating her ride with Freddy. It seemed ages since she had been on a horse, and she longed for nothing more than a good, hard romp in the open air. She was counting on it to wipe away the stubbornly persistent gloom that had been with her since her latest confrontation with the duke. Just the memory of the insulting perusal he had made of her body the day before made her hands clench.

At least this morning she was free of the possibility of encountering her employer's hateful presence. From his not so subtle words of the day before, Catherine felt quite sure he had spent the night away from home. An image of Lady Blanche rose in her mind, but Catherine refused to think on it very long. She was determined not to let anyone or anything associated with the duke bother her.

Catherine was helping herself to a second of Chef Frenier's special breakfast rolls when a noise at the door caused her to raise her eyes. When it swung open, she muttered an oath she had learned from old Jon. It seemed an added insult that, not only did her employer appear when she had been certain he was not home, but he looked magnificent even as he was so disobliging. Breakfast being an informal occasion, the duke was not wearing a coat or a cravat, only a white shirt of thin cambric material. The shirt was open at the neck, revealing a very masculine chest, and Catherine found it ridiculously difficult to pull her eyes from the sight. He must just that moment have left his toilette, for his black hair was still damp, though a stray lock had already fallen onto his brow. As always, his gray eyes were vivid and were staring back at her inscrutably. Catherine reminded herself, a little sourly perhaps, that handsome is as handsome does.

The Duke of Clarendon, unexpectedly catching sight of his employee, felt a remarkably similar, grudging admiration.

Her long chestnut hair, caught by a ribbon at the neck, tumbled in a dark, fiery mass down her back, drawing the eye to the chocolate-brown riding habit she wore. Cut in a severe military style, the habit acted as a foil for her willowy curves, and its dark color showed off her creamy complexion. He noted that her beautiful amber eyes were regarding him from beneath her thick lashes, their expression wary. Justifiably wary, he thought grimly, a picture of her sitting so prettily on Charles Musgrave's phaeton flashing before his eyes.

When the Duke gave his breakfast order, he took his seat, his eyes returning to Catherine. "Dressed for your ride with Freddy, I see," he commented before she could gather her wits to tell him of her visit to Honorine. "I wonder if you shall find him as pleasant as Charles."

Instantly angry color stained Catherine's cheeks. He had not even the decency to wish her good morning before insulting her. "I am sure I shall, your grace." Her eyes flashed at him defiantly. "Freddy seems a very pleasant fellow. He has been your closest friend for quite some time, I believe?"

The mockery in the duke's smile deepened, and he saluted her with a slight inclination of his head.

"How astute you are, Catherine. Yes, he is my closest friend, and is very loyal. I daresay you won't find Freddy easy game."

"I daresay not, your grace. But how kind you are to wish to save me the trouble of finding out for myself. Perhaps I should present you a list of all the eligible gulls I have met, and you could indicate who is and who is not loyal, or equally important, who would or would not be prepared to face your wrath to marry your supposed betrothed."

The duke's dark brow lifted sardonically as he replied with heavy sarcasm, "Oh, that would be easy for you, I think. Anyone with your talents could convince an eager suitor that I am hopelessly in love with another or some such thing."

Below the table, Catherine's hands clenched so tightly, her palms bore the marks of her nails the rest of the morning. Above the table, Catherine refused to let him see how his words upset her.

"Such a fertile imagination you have, your grace," she mimicked his sarcasm with some success. "However, we must put aside my concerns, for you have very neatly brought us to a point I must discuss with you."

Her employer's brow lifted in question.

Catherine nodded. "Actually, the question of whom you do or do not care for has already arisen."

Something flickered in the silver-gray eyes, but he said merely, "Oh?"

"Yes, indeed. Your Aunt Honorine was obliging enough to invite me to her home to enlighten me about your feelings for Lady Blanche Romney."

"Honorine discussed Blanche Romney with you?"

Her employer remained sprawled negligently in his chair, his legs stretched out before him, but when Catherine looked at his eyes, she saw they were regarding her intently. That look sobered her, reminding her they were not merely discussing the idle chatter of a malicious relative. They were seriously considering whether or not that relative had committed murder, and therefore it behooved her to put aside their animosity to relate the story accurately.

"She went out of her way to do so, in fact," Catherine informed him more soberly. "She sent a special message around yesterday morning, inviting me for a morning visit. I could see little purpose to the visit until she began to spew her gossip about you and Lady Romney. In the most solicitous tones she said I ought to be warned that you and Lady Blanche had had a *tendre* for each other years ago and were rumored to be involved with one another still. She could scarcely forbear adding that I would be a fool to marry a man who was carrying on an affair during his betrothal."

"And what was your response to my inestimable aunt?" he asked, not so much as an unruly eyelash confirming or denying the existence of an intimate relationship between himself and Blanche Romney.

"I informed her she was mistaken, and to prove it, I said you were so eager to wed and to start your nursery that you had asked to move our wedding date to August."

A short silence greeted her words, then he said in an oddly soft voice, "Such an inordinate interest you seem to have in my nursery, Catherine."

Catherine did not rise to the bait, if it was a bait, though she could feel her cheeks flush. Devil take the man, his scheme, and his nursery, she fumed to herself. Her voice when she spoke was clipped.

"Should the question arise, your grace, you renewed your vows of affection after the Enderby soiree. Aunt Emily accompanied me to Honorine's and may say something to you, for she was vastly pleased by the story."

She had hoped to shame him with the bit about

Aunt Emily, but he only asked her what Honorine's response had been.

"Honorine was very, very displeased," Catherine recalled. "She very much wanted to have me stalk indignantly from her excruciatingly ugly parlor to break off my engagement with you. When, instead, she was faced with the news that you would be marrying sooner than she had feared, she looked very much like a fish when it is pulled from the water, gasping for air with its eyes popping out."

Catherine heard the ghost of a chuckle issue from the head of the table. It and the satisfying memory of Honorine's contorted face made her giggle out loud, her eyes by their own accord lifting to meet the duke's. For the briefest moment Catherine could have sworn there was a warm look in her employer's eye, but if there had been, it was gone so quickly it might as well never have been. In its place was a sober, considering expression.

"You are wondering, I think, if that was the extent of Honorine's reaction, are you not?" Catherine asked after a moment.

"Yes, I am," the duke admitted. "Honorine's surprisingly open effort to interfere with my supposed marriage demonstrates she is against my marrying and is willing to stoop to malicious depths to interfere, but I am hard put to imagine her sticking a knife in my back." After a lengthy pause, the duke waved his hand in a gesture of impatience. "So, we are back at the beginning. I suppose we must continue as we are doing, trying to flush out other game, while I keep an eye on my next of kin in case my intuition proves to be wrong."

The duke's expression lightened when his gaze returned to his employee. "I congratulate you, Catherine. It was most resourceful of you to have turned the tables on Honorine. She would not be an easy person to fool."

The compliment pleased Catherine, but it did not appease her. "Talented I believe you said earlier," she reminded him, a sarcastic edge to her voice.

One eyebrow lifted mockingly, he replied, "So I did. And you are talented as well as resourceful. It is your honor I question, Catherine, not your ability as an actress."

"Hello there!" Freddy's voice boomed into the frigid silence that had fallen in the breakfast room. "Hope I'm not intruding, but I didn't think there was any need to drag Davies with me. I know the way well enough, what?"

At the sight of Freddy's red hair, set off by a deep green riding jacket and blinding yellow waistcoat, the anger the duke's wounding words had sparked receded somewhat.

"Good morning, Freddy." Catherine managed to smile.

"Egad, how can you stomach such colorful splendor at this hour?" The duke grimaced sourly.

Freddy completely ignored the unkind greeting, beaming instead at Catherine. "I see you look every inch as lovely first thing in the morning as last thing in the evening, Catherine. Knew those cheekbones weren't a trick of candlelight, but I couldn't be sure about the incredible color of your eyes."

Catherine acknowledged the effusive compliment with a grin, though she watched the duke's reaction out of the corner of her eye. She need not have concerned herself, for he merely made a low grumbling sound.

"Stow it, Freddy. I am not up to such a rig at this hour. And at the risk of wounding Catherine's feelings, I will add that I know the reason you've come early is not to see her, but to help yourself to Frenier's breakfast rolls, so have a seat."

Freddy accepted with such alacrity that Catherine

smiled, but she had no desire, with the duke's last comment still echoing in her mind, to remain while Freddy finished his serving. "I'll just go get my hat, Freddy," she excused herself, and waving both men to keep their seats, she escaped without once looking toward the head of the table.

16

"Freddy, do you know what mount Adam wants me to take?" Catherine asked when Freddy joined her in the front hall, the duke nowhere in sight. "I forgot to ask him before I left to collect my hat."

Freddy took in the charming little hat with a long, curling black plume that was sitting at a rakish angle on Catherine's head. "And a nice little thing it is, too," he remarked admiringly. "As to your mount, you have a surfeit of riches there. I brought a mount for you, because I knew Adam had nothing in his stables for a lady. Hasn't had since his mother died. There's been no need, because Aunt Em don't care for riding. But damn me if Adam hadn't already gone out and found something for you. He said she's a spirited filly, but he thought that might suit you."

Freddy had turned away to watch the grooms who were approaching with their mounts, and as a consequence, he missed the flash of gold in Catherine's eyes. She could just hear the duke's mocking drawl declare that a spirited filly would suit her. No doubt he thought all women should, as Blanche Romney probably did, prefer not to ride at all but be driven wherever they wanted to go.

Catherine's annoyed thoughts did not last beyond her first view of the sleek little chestnut filly that was to be hers. The dainty animal's gleaming coat was marked by four perfectly matched white stockings and a white blaze on her forehead, and when she was brought to Catherine, she shook her head as if to greet her new mistress. When had the duke found her? it occurred to Catherine to wonder. He had not known she cared to ride until after their quarrel, but surely he had not bought her such a magnificent mount then.

"Ready?" Freddy yelled to her, and she gave up her pointless musing to trot down the drive after him. When they reached the park, Catherine's face lit with a wide smile. "Thank you, Freddy," she exclaimed delightedly. "This is just what I needed. I can't believe how different the place looks without all the people. I didn't even notice the long rolling lawns yesterday, there were so many bodies strolling there."

"And your filly suits you, I think?" Freddy asked, smiling back.

"She's a beauty. How could I not like her?"

"Adam hoped she wouldn't be too much horse for you, and I see she's not."

"Do you know her name, Freddy? I was so stunned to be given her on such short notice, I quite forgot to ask."

"Adam said her owner had named her Circe, but—"

"Circe!" Catherine fairly shrieked the word, startling her horse. For several moments Catherine was diverted by the need to control her mount. When she had done so, she turned blazing eyes to Freddy. "Circe," Catherine exclaimed once more. "And do you, Freddy, know who Circe was?"

A clearly startled Freddy allowed that he did not in fact have any idea who Circe was, but added unnecessarily, "Though whoever she was, it's clear you've a bee in your bonnet over it."

"I should hope so!" was the hot reply, and Catherine proceeded to tell the startled Freddy just what the name meant. "Circe was an enchantress who lured Odysseus' sailors to their deaths. Imagine naming your mount after such a person! Only the sort of man who believes beautiful women are all dangerous and untrustworthy would do such a thing. And I refuse to countenance such a pigheaded view of women. I declare I shall name my horse after Penelope, Odysseus' faithful wife, for I believe a woman can be loyal as well as beautiful."

Catherine looked belligerently at Freddy, as if she expected him to deny her last statement, but Freddy had none of the duke's challenging manner. Upon seeing an expression made in equal parts of amazement, consternation, and alarm, Catherine was forced to laugh.

"Oh, Freddy, can you forgive me that outburst? I am afraid it was not really meant for you."

"When you ask with a smile like that, I believe I could forgive you anything," he assured her gallantly, then he chuckled. "I'll enjoy watching you and Adam together over the years. It's a good thing you're not some simpering miss; he's far too strong for that kind of wife. He needs someone with strong opinions, like you."

Catherine gave a snort, but saved herself the need for more articulate comment by urging her horse into a canter. To her great delight, Penelope, as Freddy later remarked, was a "neat little goer." At Catherine's touch she moved immediately into a smooth, floating canter. Revelling in that moment, Catherine forgot the duke, forgot they would not be sparring in the years to come, forgot that he had likely named her horse Circe himself. She was only aware of the filly's fine gait, of the wind on her face, and of the bright, lovely day.

When Freddy at last slowed their rush, her eyes were sparkling with joy. "Let's do this every day,

Freddy," she cried. "I don't think I could ever get
enough."

Freddy smiled, pleased to see her pleasure. "I
should be more than delighted to accompany you as
often as possible. You'll see, though, when you get
into the social swing, that you won't feel like arising
every morning, no matter how glorious the day. If
you've been dancing until three, riding at nine becomes less a pleasure than a duty."

"Well, perhaps you are right." Catherine's dimple
appeared."Shall I really dance until three, Freddy?
It seems such a romantic thing to dance the entire
night away."

"Not romantic at all if your feet hurt, as mine
generally do," Freddy observed with a groan.

Catherine grinned at her companion's lugubrious
expression and remarked that Freddy only had himself to blame. "If you were married or even betrothed, you wouldn't have to spend so much time
making the rounds."

Freddy's face took on a comical look of horror as
he replied that sore feet were hardly sufficient reason to get himself "all leg-shackled."

"I say, hello there! Been hailing you for a moment
now, but you are enjoying yourselves so much, you
could not hear me."

Catherine recognized the Marquess of Lynsford's
voice before she turned to greet him. She was not at
all pleased to have him intrude on her morning,
and her reserved greeting was a reflection of that
displeasure.

"I see, Miss Asterley, that the morning agrees with
you." The marquess's pale eyes regarded Catherine
with open admiration, and oblivious to Catherine's
reserve, he added with a gallant bow, "Your cheeks
put the rose to shame while your eyes outshine the
sun."

The flowery praises struck Catherine as absurd.

"You are too kind, my lord. You will turn my head with such praises; save them, I beg you, for this lovely filly. She is the duke's gift to me."

"Very lovely." The marquess, Catherine saw, was not looking at Penelope at all. His extremely warm regard made her uneasy. She glanced at Freddy, but he was bidding the marquess good day in civil tones, his countenance showing nothing to indicate the marquess was overstepping his bounds. Nevertheless, Catherine cut short the pleasantries, giving an errand for Lady de Maine as her excuse.

"Before you go, Miss Asterley," the marquess detained her. "I should like to claim the honor of a dance with you tomorrow at Almack's. I would be desolated not to partner the most beautiful lady present."

There was nothing Catherine could do but accept. When he was out of earshot, Catherine frowned upon her escort. "I cannot like that man, Freddy, and I do not know exactly why. His sister, whom I met with Charles Musgrave, seemed very nice, but her brother's extravagant praises set my teeth on edge. Tell me what you know of him."

Freddy cocked his head, thinking. "Their mother died at Anne's birth, I believe, and their father shot himself soon after. He'd lost almost everything they had, which had been considerable, at cards. Much of it in a single game, I think the story goes, though it was well before my time and I wouldn't swear to it. Afterward they had to scrape, and Lynsford won some back at cards, but borrowed more, if rumor is correct. They're an old family, you know, take an inordinate amount of pride in their history, especially Lynsford. He wants Lady Anne to restore the family fortunes with a brilliant match, but she's not the sort to put herself forward, and I understand he's been bitter over her failure. He was in an uncommonly gallant mood today, but it wasn't your fault. I mean, you didn't encourage him to wax poetic over you. It's only that you are uncommonly beautiful, which you cannot help."

Catherine responded to Freddy's words with a sigh. "Freddy, shall I tell you a little secret?" she asked, and when he nodded, she continued, "Until quite recently I did not know that I look in any way out of the ordinary."

The outrageous surprise that appeared on Freddy's plump face, brought a little half-smile to Catherine's lips.

"It's true," she assured him. "I grew up in a very isolated place with no one about to remark on my looks at all. Since I left home, however, I have been told repeatedly in both friendly and unfriendly tones that I am beautiful. And, while I suppose it is not the worst thing in the world to be thought beautiful, I have often found that it is a great deal more trouble than it is worth."

17

*T*he rooms were a good deal less grand than she had expected, there being little in the way of decoration, but Catherine decided the company on her first visit to Almack's was every bit as glittering as she had imagined it would be. Ladies dressed in silks and satins, their jewels sparkling in the light of the thousands of candles illuminating the rooms, talked or danced with gentlemen resplendent in the most formal evening attire.

Surreptitiously, Catherine wiggled toes encased in tiny slippers that were dyed to match her high-waisted bronze-colored silk gown. Her aching feet were a revelation, for she had not expected to dance so much. To appease the duke she had adopted a polite but distinctly aloof air toward all the young men pressing her to dance. Evidently, though she was not as vivacious as she had been at the Enderbys', her beauty remained unaffected, or perhaps it was that her air of reserve intrigued. Whatever the reason, she had not sat out one dance all evening. Fatigued beyond words, she had finally taken matters in her own hands and asked Freddy, after their dance together, to escort her to Lady Anne Lynsford's side.

"I hope you won't mind my settling beside you like this, but I did want to talk to you again." Catherine smiled at the quiet girl.

Lady Anne replied that the pleasure was hers, and soon, put at ease by Catherine's easy manner and sparkling smile, she was chatting comfortably. Though she had come out the Season before, Lady Anne had, like Catherine, lived most of her life in the country and found life in town more trial than pleasure.

"I do miss my long walks and finding a spot to sit comfortably reading. I hope it does not shock you, Catherine, that I enjoy reading?" Lady Anne smiled shyly at her new friend.

"Indeed not!" Catherine grinned in return. "And I confess I share your vice. Yes," she said, nodding firmly. "Why only yesterday I quite undid Freddy by revealing a knowledge of classical myths." Catherine's recounting of how her horse came to be named Penelope, complete with Freddy's bemused expression, sent Anne into a fit of the giggles.

When their laughter died away, Catherine continued more softly. "Nor am I surprised you prefer the country to town. A mutual friend of ours, Lord Charles Musgrave, has admitted a similar preference to me." When Lady Anne's cheek colored rapidly, Catherine squeezed her hand and explained quickly how she had come to learn of their regard for each other.

"If you will agree to it, I would like to help," Catherine's eyes danced with mischief. "Why could we not go riding together and take only my groom? It is not so unusual, and if we are early enough, there will be no one to see us meet Sir Charles. You mustn't think you will put me out. I want to do it. Sir Charles loves you very much, and it hurts me to see such genuine affection thwarted for the most selfish of reasons."

Lady Anne looked at Catherine half-frightened by her spirit. "I am scarcely able to believe I have someone to confide in. I hardly know what to say, Miss Asterley," she confessed after a few moments.

"It will be my pleasure to be your friend," Catherine assured the shy young woman beside her. "But if we are to be friends, then you must call me Catherine. Miss Asterley sounds far too formal for friends."

Lady Anne smiled in earnest at that. "I should like that very much, Catherine," she said sincerely. "And you will call me Anne?"

"Agreed." Catherine nodded her confirmation of their friendship. "Now, what about my plan? Do you think Lynsford will allow you to ride with me?"

A bitter laugh jarred the air. "In truth, I do not know," Anne admitted. "For most of my life my brother took no notice of me, considering me too drab for a true Lynsford. But when he insisted I have a London Season to make a brilliant—his word, you understand—match, he became more of a watch-dog. I am lucky that he believes Charles offered for me because he needed a wife, not out of affection. If he thought we loved each other, he would prevent any association between us, even at dances. But, because he thinks Charles' interest is only perfunctory, he allows us an occasional meeting. I'm sure he thinks it enhances my desirability with others if I am seen to have a partner." When Lady Anne's lip trembled again, she was forced to stop for a moment before she added in the most forlorn voice Catherine had ever heard, "Oh, Catherine, I love Charles so much. I cannot tell you how difficult it is to act indifferently toward him when Lynsford is around."

"It is absurd that you should have to," Catherine snapped, her sympathetic heart outraged. "At least when you meet him on our rides, you won't have to worry about your brother."

Lady Anne's fine hazel eyes began to sparkle at the thought. "We shall be so indebted to you, Catherine," she cried.

"Nonsense!" was the brisk reply. "It will be my pleasure, for I am fond of you both. But for heaven's sake, Anne, you mustn't look so grateful or the entire assembly will know something is afoot."

Catherine's mock outrage caused Lady Anne to laugh again, and thus, to Catherine's relief, they presented a picture of innocent camaraderie to the man she had noticed approaching them.

"What a pleasure to find you with Anne, Miss Asterley. She is sorely in need of stimulating company."

Catherine did not fail to note that, upon her brother's appearance, Lady Anne shrank back.

"You must not tease so, Lord Lynsford. I have found Lady Anne to be most enjoyable company. I vow I've not enjoyed most of my partners half so much."

The marquess's pale eyes glittered strangely for a moment, and Catherine was hard put not to shiver with distaste. "I take that as a challenge, Miss Asterley," he said. "I believe you will find my company at least as pleasurable as my sister's. You did promise to dance with me."

Much as she disliked him, Catherine did not want to offend him, and with a nice if not dazzling smile she held him back before rising to dance.

"Lord Lynsford, I have a favor to ask of you. I beg you will allow Lady Anne to accompany me for a morning ride in the park occasionally. I should dearly love to find a friend of my own age and sex in London."

A pleased smile crossed Lynsford's face, and Catherine could almost hear Anne breathe a sigh of relief. "I would be pleased to allow Anne to associate with you. You do us both a great honor."

Catherine, murmuring that the honor was all hers, wished that Lynsford might learn to be less extravagant in his praise, and she hoped he did not imagine that her interest in his sister indicated an interest in him.

"And you are to marry at Christmas, Miss Asterley?" the marquess asked once they were on the floor.

"We've advanced the date to August," she corrected casually.

"Oh, I beg your pardon. I am not usually so clumsy," the marquess exclaimed apologetically, for he had stepped on Catherine's foot. "Well," he said when they had resumed their dance, "who could blame Clarendon for rushing things with a woman like you waiting?"

It occurred to Catherine that the marquess's smile was oddly strained, but Catherine, having just found the duke's narrowed gaze upon her, was too distraught to pay the marquess much attention. She looked again at the duke and saw he was in the company of a heavyset, elderly gentleman. She advanced a little to the left in the steps of the dance and saw that Blanche Romney, her voluptuous figure displayed in a clinging blue silk gown, was the third person in the duke's group. An unsteady bubble of laughter almost burst from her. Aunt Emily had understated the fact when she had called Lord Romney unprepossessing; he was dreadful. No wonder Blanche was interested in Clarendon. A sudden thought lightened Catherine's mood. Perhaps it was Lord Romney's presence that had caused the duke to look so displeased, and not something she had done.

In the milling throng at the end of the dance she lost sight of the duke and consequently was surprised when she saw Lynsford had escorted her directly to him. The Romneys had departed, as had the duke's narrowed look, though the coolness of his greeting to Lynsford did not augur well.

"My compliments, Clarendon, on your choice of brides. Miss Asterley is quite without match. I trust you do not object to my asking her to dance." The marquess's words seemed unobjectionable, but an odd challenge in his tone caught Catherine's attention. Looking at him quickly, she was disconcerted to discover an air of tense excitement about him.

Clarendon seemed unaware of anything unusual and regarded the other man with an impassive expression that held only a faint hint of distaste.

"Not at all, Lynsford," he replied smoothly. "Catherine is quite capable, I am sure, of determining the sort of company she wishes to keep." Throwing a mocking smile her way, he bowed. "I think it is time I claimed my rights." The tautness of the muscles in the arm he extended to her caused Catherine to hope for a dance whose steps would take her to the opposite end of the floor from her partner.

"I would not have thought Lynsford was the sort to interest you. He's a pauper, you know," Clarendon commented after a moment.

Catherine's eyes flashed, but with an effort she reminded herself where she was. "It is his sister who interests me, not the marquess," Catherine replied coldly.

"A dance and a chat are not marks of interest?" the duke inquired, his tone so highly skeptical it sneered.

Catherine took a deep breath. "He asked me for the dance yesterday in the park. There was no way I could refuse him and not cause embarrassment. Ask Freddy if you don't believe me. Besides," Catherine went on, "I do not believe the marquess asked me to dance for the pleasure of my company."

The duke's eyes lifted with surprise. "And what makes you believe that the marquess alone in all the room is immune to your charms?"

"You are mocking me, but it does not signify." Catherine tossed her head, ignoring for the moment that her employer was most certainly in the room. "I do not know the why of it. I can only tell you what I see. You sparked more feeling in him than I. He was almost daring you to challenge him when he asked if you objected to our dance. Besides," Catherine added with an air of finality, "his smile is not genuine. It does not reach his eyes."

At her words, the duke, quite unexpectedly, gave a soft chuckle. "Such a telling thing," he said, his voice dry.

For several moments their eyes clashed, Catherine's hotly defiant look met by the duke's cool, mocking stare. Just as she thought she could not bear it a moment longer, the musicians began to play.

To Catherine's distress she recognized the notes of a waltz. It would be the first she had ever danced. She had not imagined they would be so close, and when the duke's arm moved to circle her waist, she stiffened. It reminded her strongly of the feel of his body tight against hers the night of their quarrel.

"Will you unbend a little, if I allow I believe you are sincere?" the duke asked after a moment.

Not at all certain she was stiff because of their argument over Lynsford, Catherine replied, staring into his shoulder, which was at eye level, "It will be an unusual and welcome experience to be thought sincere, your grace."

"To tell you the truth," he said, and Catherine felt his broad shoulders shrug, "I also thought Lynsford's manner odd, though why it should be, I have no idea, I've scarcely ever spoken with him."

Catherine, concentrating on her steps, made no reply and they were silent until the duke suddenly leaned back to look at her. "This is your first waltz," he said flatly.

"Yes. Am I so awkward?" Catherine's wide amber eyes flew up to his.

"Not awkward," he answered, regarding her with his heavy-lidded gaze. "Merely unpracticed. After one has danced the waltz enough, there is little reason to concentrate as hard as you are doing." His eyes flicking to her soft lower lip, he added, "You give yourself away when you bite your lip like that. It's a habit you have when you concentrate."

An unwanted blush heated her cheeks. What a small detail to have noticed. She was not given any time to dwell on the thought, however, for when the duke pulled her close again, she became insidiously aware how intoxicating the rhythm of the music was, and then slowly, very slowly, she became conscious how well she fit in his strong arms. Dancing the waltz was like floating, she thought dreamily, her body feeling light as a feather.

"That's it," she heard the duke's low voice murmur softly above her.

18

After Almack's the social whirl, as Clarendon had predicted, caught the inhabitants of Clarendon House in an unrelenting grip. Every day Catherine and Lady de Maine retired to the morning room, where Davies brought them a staggering pile of invitations to routs, balls, assemblies, teas, breakfasts, card parties, and soirees. Catherine would take up each invitation and read it aloud to Lady de Maine, who would to Catherine's delight indicate with an imperial wave of her thumb whether or not the invitation was to be considered.

At each of these affairs, Catherine was surrounded by a crowd of young people, among whom there were now almost as many young women as young men. The young ladies of the *ton* had at first held back from Catherine, afraid another vain beauty had come to preen before them. As time passed, however, they began to realize Catherine was astonishingly unconcerned with her looks and consequently never made them feel less-favored. Of almost equal importance, they soon discovered her to be a good listener who never repeated what was whispered to her in confidence. She would listen patiently while they poured out their woes, and if it was in her power to do something to help, she did. Netty Barbridge, for example, when that young lady had complained she lacked the ability to know what colors would compliment her somewhat sallow complexion, was invited to accompany Catherine and Lady de Maine shopping, as Catherine correctly believed Aunt Emily would be delighted to assist.

At the moment, in the midst of Lady Clarice Hensley's rout, Catherine was engaged in a similar, though more frustrating, effort. Several days before at the lending library Miss Amelia Smythe-Keatting had tearfully confessed she was head over heels in love with Mr. John Newlinburry, who, since Catherine's advent, had forgotten all about her. Feeling absurdly responsible, Catherine had agreed to reintroduce the pair and, with Mr. Newlinburry on her arm, was as subtly as possible making for young Miss Amelia. Unfortunately, she had encountered a series of frustrating interruptions to the progress of her plan. One of these was the Marquess of Lynsford, whose string of extravagant compliments almost sent Mr. Newlinburry scurrying. Catherine prevented him from leaving, however, by the simple expedient of holding on to his arm. Just as it looked as if Mr. Newlinburry would outlast the marquess, Eustace, with consummate ill-timing, waddled up.

Catherine bit her lip impatiently while Eustace exchanged idle conversation with the marquess and Mr. Newlinburry. Then, to her relieved surprise, Eustace, after a passing remark of Lynsford's about the opera, turned a vile shade of puce and left on the instant. Her attention had not been on the conversation, so Catherine did not know exactly what had been said, but neither did she much care. Other matters were on her mind, and her only thought at present was to excuse herself and Mr. Newlinburry from the marquess. She did so after a few more moments by explaining she had promised the young man the honor of escorting her to the punch bowl. While she firmly marched him to it, Catherine begged Mr. Newlinburry to forgive her lie, declaring she really was dying of thirst. Puffed up at being pre-

ferred to a marquess, the young man stammered his
complete understanding and arrived at the punch
bowl, where to everyone's surprise Miss Smythe-
Keatting was also obtaining a refreshment. After a
few moments, her blushing interest and Catherine's
adamant silence turned Mr. Newlinburry's attention
to Miss Amelia, allowing Catherine to thankfully
depart.

"Now, that's a trick Penelope might have used. If
she'd paired off each of her pesky suitors with some
willing young lady, your heroine could have saved
herself a great deal of trouble."

Catherine's nerves jumped as she looked into the
duke's amused eyes. They always did when she first
saw him. It was the way she readied herself to deflect
his slighting comments on her actress's wiles. At every event they attended he kept an insulting watch
over her, and if she laughed lightly at some young
gallant's remarks, she could be sure to find his derisive regard upon her, or if she danced the waltz with
another, she would see his brow creased in a dark
glare. It was his pithy, scorching remarks that she
dreaded the most, however, and she tried to prepare
herself for them.

Apprehension, surprisingly, was not the only fac-
tor in her response to her employer, a fact she both
recognized and bemoaned. One lady, unaware that
Catherine stood nearby, had with an unusual light in
her eye for so matronly a figure, described the Duke
of Clarendon to a friend as magnetic. Catherine had
had to agree. It was the quality that turned all eyes
toward him when he entered a room. It was the
quality that, despite his infuriating treatment of her,
made her heart race when he approached for the
one waltz he invariably claimed as his.

Familiarity, had it been allowed a chance to oper-
ate, might have dulled her response to her dark,
handsome employer, though Catherine doubted it,

but familiarity had not been allowed the chance to grow up between them. Clarendon had seen to that. Since her debut at Almack's, the duke had successfully avoided being entirely alone with her. He had not again joined her for breakfast. He never rode with her, never accompanied her to the lending library, never drove with her in the park, nor even took tea with her, unless Lady de Maine, Freddy, or half the *ton* were present as well. Of course, as part of their masquerade, he was obliged to seek her out at public functions, and Catherine supposed that was his intent this time. He had come for their "betrothed duty," as Catherine had privately dubbed their public tête-à-têtes.

"You needn't look so braced, Catherine." Clarendon eyed his silent companion with a half-smile. "I am only making an effort to demonstrate that I notice the good as well as the bad."

Catherine's wits returned then, and she opened her mouth to retort that he had given her precious little cause to think so, but the duke, putting a finger on her lips, forbade her to speak unkindly.

He said something about it being time to act as lovers, but Catherine scarcely heard him. She was far too distracted by the feel of his light touch on her lips. When he removed his hand, it was as if the world had turned right side up again, and she became aware that he was still speaking.

"I see I must prove myself. Only last week I observed you matching up young Saint-Giles with that whey-faced chit, I forget her name."

"Constance Whittington," Catherine said, her eyes still reflecting uncertainty, for she was not at all sure what he was leading up to.

"Ah, yes, how could I forget? Constance and she will be most constantly chattering, if the first eighteen years of her life are any indication."

Catherine's mouth twitched at that, for Constance Whittington was indeed a chatterbox.

"Yes, I see you agree."

Catherine found it remarkably difficult to avoid the duke's eyes and impossible not to smile in response to the twinkle she detected there.

"So," the duke continued after a moment spent watching Catherine's engaging smile curve her soft mouth, "there are two of your admirers painstakingly bestowed upon other more willing arms. It is a puzzle, you know. It is not, I think, customary for an object of admiration to so assiduously seek to deflect it."

Catherine shrugged her indifference to the customary and, still wondering where the knife lay hidden in his words, perversely sought to anticipate it herself. "You misunderstand, your grace. Doing so rids me of the nuisance of tripping over another fatuous face."

"No." He solemnly shook his head. "I think you underestimate yourself. I think the fact is, you, Miss Catherine, have a generous heart."

"Generous heart!" Catherine gaped inelegantly at the unexpected praise. Her employer, his mouth quirking ever so slightly, tapped her chin, thus reminding that her mouth was hanging open. Catherine closed it with a snap.

"Shall we play an echo game?" he asked, a not entirely mocking amusement gleaming in his eyes. "You do know the word 'generous'? It could have described you when you made every effort to put a little Irish maid at ease or braved my not inconsiderable wrath in a doomed effort to save Aunt Emily's feelings. Or it could refer to the way you tenaciously held Mr. Newlinburry at your side while making your way to the eagerly waiting Miss Smythe-Keatting."

"Actresses are self-serving," Catherine paraphrased him stiffly, still unrelenting.

"There is no need to be so touchy," he chided, the laughter in his gray eyes riveting her. "I am only paying tribute where tribute is due. I admit that I am surprised and that my surprise does stem from my, ah, acquaintance with several actresses. But— and this should appease you a little—they were no less generous in this sense than most society beauties I have known."

Catherine was truly not certain what to say, the novelty of receiving the duke's praise rendering her speechless. Still, however surprising his mood might be, it was also irresistible, and convincing herself it would do no harm to enjoy so rare a moment, Catherine, for the first time in many weeks, deliberately prolonged a conversation with her employer.

"Thank you for your kind words, your grace. They are as welcome as they are . . . surprising. But I am a poor subject for discussion; we shall either run out of things to say too soon or fall into an argument. There is one topic, however, in which we both share an interest. I wonder if you have learned anything new concerning your brother's death?"

The duke eyed her a moment as if he might take exception to what she had said, before, with a slight inclination of his head, he gracefully accepted the abrupt change in the conversation. "Actually, I do have news that I have been intending to tell you." He raised his head and, seeing no one close by, turned his silver-gray gaze back to Catherine. "Sometime ago I hired a man, Mr. Brown, to make some inquiries in the area around Clarendon Hall while we played our parts here. Interestingly enough, he has learned there was a stranger in the vicinity at the time of Gerald's death. Even more interesting is the fact that the stranger left the area the very day of the murder and has not been seen there since. Mr. Brown is tracking the man now, and I hope to have news of his success soon."

"How is Mr. Brown able to trace him? Did he have some distinguishing feature?" Catherine asked.

The duke's white teeth flashed. "Well, he was not immensely fat, if that is your question."

"It would have made matters simpler, you must allow." Catherine, still wary with him, looked away.

"Indeed it would," the duke agreed. "And he has obliged us by having a distinctive, crescent-shaped scar on his left cheek. But the scar is particularly intriguing because he was smooth of cheek when he appeared in the village. No one took much notice of him at first; he called himself a tinkerer and had a few ribbons and threads to sell out of his wagon. Jennings, the tavern owner, knew him on sight, for it seems the stranger came there once or twice for a pint. The day of Gerald's death, actually just two hours after it, Jennings met the stranger leaving town. The heavens had opened in a mighty downpour, and Jennings found him trying to push his wagon out of a muddy rut. Being a helpful sort, Jennings lent him a hand. When the wagon was freed, the stranger thanked him, and Jennings had the opportunity to notice the scar on his cheek. Jennings swears that, though he never noticed the scar before, from the look of it that afternoon, it was not a new scar."

"He must have tried to cover it up, because he didn't want to be singled out," Catherine cried, her eyes dancing with excitement.

"Perhaps," was all the encouragement her employer would give her, his interest apparently on the sparkle in her eyes.

"Well, I think so," replied Catherine, not noticing how closely her employer was regarding her. "Has Mr. Brown been able to trace the man very far, your grace?"

"He has followed him to London. He has a lead or

two on him here, but has not yet been able to locate
him."

When at last the duke escorted her to Aunt Emily,
whose friend, Mrs. Jarred, was eager to regale them
with the story of her trip to India to visit her young-
est son working there with the East India Company, Catherine made a great show of her interest,
though her heart was not in it. As Mrs. Jarred talked,
Catherine was sobering and, as a result, chiding herself for caring even a little about the duke's praise.
Angrily she pointed out to herself that for the past
month and more she had been subjected to baseless
accusations, dark glares, mocking, derisive glances,
and arbitrary demands, and she had learned nothing
from it at all. Instead, at the least kind word, she
turned to putty, forgetting herself so much as to
deliberately prolong their conversation.

With a great effort, Catherine brought her attention back to Mrs. Jarred, reminding herself that it
never served any purpose to dwell upon the Duke of
Clarendon. More instructive, if less interesting, would
be to lose herself in the exotic world Mrs. Jarred
described.

19

"Catherine!" Anne Lynsford burst into the morning room, where Catherine could often be found enjoying a book in the sunshine. Over the past weeks the two girls had become good friends. Riding twice a week to meet Charles and visiting together in the afternoon at Clarendon House had given them time to know each other and to like what they saw. However, Catherine, after one look at Anne's pale face, could tell this was to be no ordinary visit.

"I am not certain what to do, Catherine." Anne's large eyes were fixed on her friend, while her hand nervously pleated her dress. "Lynsford joined me for tea yesterday, which is extremely unusual for him, you know how he avoids me." Catherine heard the bitter note in her friend's voice and had to restrain herself from damning Lynsford aloud. "Then, after a few lowering remarks on my looks, he began to question me about our rides. Oh, my dear, I tried to maintain an innocent air, answering all his questions as honestly as I could, but I was so nervous, I am sure I gave it all away."

"What sort of things did he want to know?" Catherine asked, striving to remain calm.

"Where we rode, when, who accompanied us, whether or not anyone met us."

"Did he ask about Charles?"

"No, but that means little. He would not want to warn me of his suspicions." Lady Anne frowned a moment, her expression perplexed. "He seemed particularly interested in how many grooms accompany us and whether or not Clarendon comes. He asked several times if the duke had ever met us, even by chance. I have no idea why he should care, but you can never tell with my brother. He may be disguising his true intent, or he may be concerned for our safety. Of one thing I am certain: his interest was not idle curiosity. He has something in mind and I am so afraid that it is Charles."

Catherine watched helplessly as Anne tried to still the trembling of her lips. It distressed her greatly that there was little she could say or do to comfort her friend. It was obvious they would have to give up their rides for a while at least, and should Anne be correct, perhaps forever.

"I can't meet Charles again until I know about Lynsford," Anne's troubled voice echoed Catherine's thoughts. "But I can't just cut it off without meeting him once more. If you'll agree to come, we could go tomorrow, and I'll explain. It won't be so bad if I've had the chance to say good-bye."

"Of course you want to see him once more," Catherine assured her friend staunchly. "And I shall be pleased to be at your door at eight o'clock sharp."

"Oh, Catherine, you are the dearest friend!" Lady Anne embraced her gratefully. "But I must impose on you still more, if you will let me?"

"Impose, no. Help, of course, you goose," Catherine disentangled herself from Anne's arms with a laugh.

"Will you arrange the meeting with Charles?" Anne asked, the first signs of happiness dawning in her hazel eyes. "I don't think I should speak with him tonight, the better to throw my brother off the scent, but I've no way to arrange things without you."

"If I am smiling after I chat with him, you'll know he can come. If not ... well, I cannot imagine he won't be there, even if he has to break his neck in the effort."

Anne blushed lightly at Catherine's words, and Catherine grinned, pleased to see her friend shed some of her anxiety.

"Well, look who's here!" Lady de Maine exclaimed with pleasure when she saw Anne. "I declare there could not be a more fetching sight in all London, do you think, Adam?"

A quick flutter of Catherine's stomach muscles confirmed that Clarendon had indeed accompanied his aunt and had paused to look at the two girls framed in the morning-room window. They made, as Lady de Maine had said, a fetching sight. Lady Anne was not a great beauty by any means, but her sweet nature showed in her large eyes and heart-shaped mouth. Her soft sandy-brown hair had been dressed in pretty ringlets, and the rose color of her muslin afternoon dress put some needed color in her cheeks. It was only natural, however, that the viewer's eye would soon be drawn to the girl by her side. Catherine's rich hair, soft skin, and flawless features made her a beauty, but it was the life in her expressive, unusual amber eyes that made her an exceptional one. Today the dark green of the muslin dress she wore deepened their color, making them gleam all the more.

"Very pretty," the duke murmured, bowing slightly to both girls, his eyes coming to rest on Catherine.

"I declare, Crowell's excursion was extraordinary. Have you ever seen such," Lady de Maine exclaimed, settling herself in her customary seat next to Catherine. She referred to a breakfast they had attended the day before at Lord Crowell's estate an hour's ride from London. Like others of his class, Lord Crowell was a collector, but unlike the others, he collected exotic animals rather than *objects d'art*. At least two hundred of the *ton*'s most select members had been invited to view the result of his efforts and enjoy a sumptuous breakfast served, Catherine was amused to note, in the late afternoon.

"I think I enjoyed the monkeys the most," Lady Anne responded shyly. Remembering something, however, she glanced at Catherine, a giggle erupting from her.

"A fine friend you are." Catherine glared at her friend's laughter, though her own lips twitched.

"And what is behind all this giggling?" Lady de Maine smiled at the two girls. "I believe there's a joke on Catherine."

Still laughing, Anne turned to Lady de Maine. "Something like that, my lady. Catherine and Freddy and I were on our way to see the monkeys when Catherine's most ardent admirer, Lord Aylesford, appeared. Aylesford is a sweet boy, my lady, but I believe you'll agree he can spout the most utter nonsense. I am afraid, knowing his interest was in Catherine, not us, Freddy and I made haste to leave, stranding Catherine with him. I don't think I'll ever forget the piercing look she shot us. Though"—Anne turned twinkling eyes on her friend—"Catherine, if she had not such a generous heart, might have dismissed him out of hand and saved herself."

"So Aylesford's plaguing you, is he?" Lady de Maine's eyes gleamed with amusement. "We could put Adam on him, if you like. That should get rid of him."

Catherine glanced at Clarendon through veiled lashes to gauge how he had taken a reference to one of her admirers. She did not think he would praise her for her "generous heart" in this instance.

"No, Aunt Em, we'll not need to bring the heavy artillery." She nodded slightly toward the duke, noting that his expression was bland, revealing little. "Aylesford is a pest, prosing on so, but he's harmless."

"I saw you tapping your pretty little foot while he

was showing you the lions, I believe," the duke lazily joined the conversation, sending Catherine's hopes for an early end to the topic into the grave. She tried hard not to think how the duke had said she had a pretty little foot; he had said it for the sake of the others. He was actually letting her know he had been watching her with the most gullible of her admirers.

"Yes, he did show me the lions," Catherine replied as if to end the matter.

"And what caused the vexation?" the duke pressed idly, his eyes not straying from hers.

Aware his interest was anything but idle, Catherine became a trifle defensive. "Lord Aylesford was making a prosy attempt to compare my eyes to those of the lioness."

"My dear, you sound so indignant." Lady de Maine smiled fondly at Catherine. "But it's true. Now that I look closely, they look only a little darker. Fancy Aylesford having such wit!"

"Wit!" Catherine cried, outraged by Aunt Emily's defection to Aylesford. "They may be something of the same color, I cannot say, for I cannot see them, but I should hope the similarity ends there. I felt it was almost an insult to have my eyes compared to that sleepy, almost vacant-looking animal."

"So that was it!" The duke threw his head back with a laugh. He was joined by both Lady de Maine and Anne, which left Catherine to regard their hilarity with more than a little exasperation sparkling in her eyes.

Looking into her indignant face, the duke grinned his full lopsided grin. "Be easy, my dear," he addressed her more softly than he had in a long, long while. "I think you have little need to worry. I have seen your eyes in many moods, from sparkling to stormy, but to my regret, I have yet to see them look the least bit sleepy."

This confidence had the effect of stunning Cath-

erine so that she was scarcely aware of the pretty
blush stealing over her cheeks. Why must he confuse
the issue between them by suddenly being so charming? Her large eyes flicked to his in hopes of answer,
then flicked away as quickly. How unnerving he could
be when his eyes were fastened on her like that, she
thought, relieved beyond words to hear the first of
their afternoon visitors arriving.

20

The next evening at Lady Kidwell's ball, Catherine was given little time at first to seek out Charles Musgrave. From the instant of her arrival, a steady line of gentlemen, young and old, solicited her hand for one dance after another, and with little pleasure she could see out of the corner of her eye one of her most persistent admirers coming to claim the next dance. Time had proved her wrong in respect to the Marquess of Lynsford. Not only did he praise her endlessly and unfailingly reserve a dance for himself, he had on more than one occasion regarded her with a distinctively possessive gleam in his eye. His attention in no way pleased Catherine. It was cloying, and the impression she had formed when she had first met him lingered. The marquess continued to remind her of a cunning, secretive fox, though his nearly colorless countenance had none of a fox's beauty.

His manner toward Clarendon was the only thing about him that had improved. He was not friendly, but neither was he challenging, almost taunting, as he had been that first night at Almack's. The duke, if he knew what lay behind the marquess's earlier tension, did not say so to Catherine, leaving her to form her own conclusions with little success.

"You are lovelier tonight than ever, Miss Asterley," Lynsford's strangely high voice extolled her.

"Please, sir." Catherine smiled briefly. "A lady can

152

only listen to a little flattery, or it will spoil her taste for plainer conversation. Tell me instead of your pursuits for the last few days. I believe we have seen little of you."

For an instant a veil dropped over the pale eyes, as if he sensed a criticism and was not pleased. "With a woman as lovely as you beside me, it is difficult to speak of myself, but perhaps it would interest you to know I have been down to look at the estates in Kent that used to belong to my family. I am hopeful that I may recover them shortly."

Surprised, for she had not thought the Lynsford finances sufficient for such a project, Catherine expressed pleasure for him. "I know, my lord, it must mean a great deal to you."

"Indeed it does." The vehemence of his response startled her, and Catherine saw that her partner, his lips twisted into a snarl, had for the moment forgotten her. But not for long.

"It is a very beautiful setting, Miss Asterley." He looked down at her, his eyes gleaming with admiration. "One worthy of a beautiful woman."

His voice held such meaning, Catherine could scarcely misunderstand. "My lord," she protested, unsure what else to say and wishing the dance would suddenly end.

"I meant no offense," he responded quickly. "You are too honorable to allow me to speak so freely while you are engaged to another, are you not?"

Catherine longed to fling at him that she did not care for his free speech, because she knew what a brute he was to his sister. But to do so would only jeopardize Anne's happiness, so she only nodded.

"But what if you were to learn, Miss Asterley, that your betrothed was unworthy of you?" the marquess asked, his pale eyes regarding her with an eager, unsettling gleam.

Catherine drew back, an expression of displeasure

on her face. "Really, sir, you presume greatly to ask such a thing!"

"Do I?" The marquess's thin lips tightened, as did the long, thin hand holding hers. There was a dangerous glitter in his pale-blue eyes, which recalled a warning of Anne's that Lynsford could become unhinged when displeased. Though she called herself every kind of coward, Catherine thought it best to let the marquess have his say.

"I care a great deal for you, Miss Asterley," Lynsford continued, his voice raspy with feeling. "You must believe that I want only the very best for you. Is that presumption? I think not. Somehow I cannot believe a lady as lovely as you must be content with another woman's leavings."

Catherine, thoroughly shocked that Lynsford would say such a coarse, ugly thing to her, tried to pull from his grasp. The marquess's grip tightened, however, and unwilling to create a scene, Catherine resumed dancing.

"I have made you angry." The marquess's voice was all apology now. "But what I have said is for your sake, Miss Asterley. I speak only the truth. Look over there, if you do not believe me."

Slowly, suspecting in advance what she would see, Catherine turned her head in the direction he indicated. Clarendon was dancing with Lady Blanche and there was a smile on his lips.

"Do you see the pendant?"

She did, of course, see the large sapphire pendant that nestled between Lady Blanche's provocatively displayed breasts. Even from this distance, Catherine could tell that it was costly.

"Rumors are disgusting things"—Lynsford's lips twisted into a thin smile—"yet I believe it is wise to be forewarned. The gossip has it that the beauteous Blanche could not charm such a costly bauble out of Romney, but Clarendon was more than willing to come up with it. I thought you should know this. Such a splendid piece of jewelry signifies, I think, more than a passing interest."

Like a snake the whispered words hissed their way into Catherine's ear, slithered around her mind, and wound themselves tightly around her heart. They hurt her for some reason she had no wish to examine. She would keep her mind on the man who had wanted to cause her that hurt. It disgusted her that Lynsford should be so eager to carry tales, and she turned a disapproving eye upon him.

"I do not believe our conversation is at all appropriate, Lord Lynsford," she rebuked him coldly. "The duke will be my husband, and I am confident of his affection. If we are to remain friends, Lord Lynsford, I must ask that you never raise this distasteful subject again."

"I see." For a split second naked fury burned in the marquess's eyes and Catherine knew exactly why Anne seemed to shrink when her brother was around. When he spoke again, however, he had mastered himself, though she could tell from the coldness of his voice that he was still very angry. "I made a mistake when I supposed you strong enough to face the truth, Miss Asterley. I see you are not. I am very disappointed in you, but I give you my word I shall never trouble you on this subject again."

After what seemed an eternity, the music ended and Catherine was freed from the marquess's distasteful touch. A stiff curtsy excused her into the company of her next partner, Mr. Grenville, a shy young man whose need to concentrate on his steps made it impossible for him to compete with the marquess's words for Catherine's attention.

Smiling serenely at her young partner, Catherine saw, not his admiring face, but a large sapphire pendant. She did not trust the marquess much. His attentions to her had been too persistent for her not

to know he would like to see her separate from
Clarendon, but in this case she did not think he had
needed to invent anything. Catherine had known
from the beginning that the duke was interested in
Blanche, and he had done nothing in the interim to
prove otherwise. The sight of him smiling into
Blanche's provocatively pouting face was not exactly
unusual, nor was it possible to ignore how often the
duke held his first love close in a waltz. Why he
should care for a woman who, though extremely
beautiful and possessed of a lush figure, had chosen
to marry another man, Catherine did not know. How
could she expect to understand, though, she who
knew so little about love.

Soon, she comforted herself, the murderer was
bound to make his move and she would be free. She
would go away from London, far from the gossip, to
a place where she would never hear of the Duke of
Clarendon, nor have to think of whom he loved and
what he gave her as a token of that love.

A heavy, leaden feeling, not relief, spread through
her at the thought. Unconsciously as she turned
around in the figure of the dance, Catherine's eyes
glanced around the room, stopping only when they
found a dark head and broad shoulders. Suddenly,
silver-gray eyes were raised to connect with hers. For
a long moment, Catherine stared from across the
room into the duke's eyes. She was aware, without
thinking on it, how handsome he was, how tall, how
assured, and how compelling. Catherine did not feel
Mr. Grenville's hand when he took hers and twirled
her about; she was not really aware of dancing at all.
A new and utterly terrifying understanding had exploded without warning in her mind.

No wonder Lynsford's ugly gossip had wounded
her so. No wonder she, who had once professed so
little use for it, had spoken so earnestly about love to

Anne. No wonder her employer had the power to send her blood singing through her veins.

No wonder, because, God help her, she was in love with him. She had fallen in love with the Duke of Clarendon, her mind repeated mechanically, as if by sheer repetition she might understand the words. How could she have fallen in love with a man so utterly beyond her reach, a man who despised her and loved another? When had it happened? She remembered the first night she had met him and how he had affected her even then.

In a daze she wondered hazily what on earth she was to do. Perhaps it was only because her mind was numb, but she could think of nothing. Escape was the only answer, and for that she must wait until her work was completed.

Catherine was still reeling from her discovery when the dance came to an end. Distractedly she thanked Mr. Grenville, her only thought to make for the ladies' retiring room to gather her wits. That respite, however, was not to be.

"It's my waltz, I believe."

The duke's low, lazy voice sent a shiver through her, a shiver made all the more intense by her new understanding of her feelings. Catherine avoided his eyes, afraid she could not hide her turbulent thoughts from him. It was imperative that he not know, for her imagination, pricking her like a thousand needles, easily conjured up the amused, mocking smile with which he would greet the knowledge that she had, despite everything, fallen a victim to his charm.

"Catherine, is something wrong?" There was genuine concern—or so it seemed—in the duke's voice, but Catherine could not bring herself to look at him directly. She was not at all sure what her reaction would be if she did. Absurdly enough, she thought she might cry.

Shaking her head in answer to his question, Catherine mumbled into his shoulder, "No, I am fine. I was only lost in thought, your grace."

"How complimentary." If there was a revealing testiness beneath the dry response, Catherine was far too preoccupied to notice such subtleties at the moment.

She was trying to put aside all thoughts of her stupendous discovery and dance as normally as possible. It did not help at all that she knew she was failing in her effort. She was too intensely aware of her partner tonight and of her feelings toward him to relax and give herself up to the pleasures of the dance. Twice she stumbled and felt his gray eyes give her a searching glance, but she kept her lashes firmly lowered, never acknowledging the errors.

The rest of the evening was a torture. It required such concentration for her to appear normal, she developed a mighty headache. Eventually she did recall her promise to Anne, however, and signaled Charles Musgrave when he came from the floor with his partner, Lady Kidwell's pretty young daughter.

"Could we get some fresh air, do you think?" Catherine asked pointedly.

"Of course. Dancing is such hot work, I agree," Charles replied with a twinkle in his eye. He led her onto the balcony, where they, as Catherine had hoped, found themselves alone.

The air was cool and for a moment they stood quietly enjoying its freshness.

"Charles," Catherine broke the silence first, "I've not the best news. Anne thinks Lynsford may suspect our rides. Can you meet us tomorrow? She wants to meet at least once more to explain and, I suspect, think what to do next."

"Damn the fellow!" The words burst from the man beside her. "Forgive me, but this situation is unbearable. I detest this secrecy, this sneaking about.

It's as if I were a boy of eighteen, not a man of thirty."

Catherine remained silent, for she knew there was no response she could make, and after a few moments, Charles gave a long sigh, conceding defeat for the moment. "Of course I'll come. As close to eight as possible?"

"Yes, at eight in the little copse by the lake."

The two stayed on the balcony a few moments longer, chatting quietly of subjects other than Anne and her brother. The interlude served to calm Catherine's nerves somewhat, and when she returned to the ballroom, she was wearing a slight but genuine smile for the first time since her dance with Lynsford.

Had she but known it, that smile had appeared most damning to a pair of watchful silver-gray eyes.

Before Catherine had asked Charles to join her on the balcony, she had looked for the duke. When she had found him to be occupied—sourly she thought it entirely appropriate that the cause of his distraction was Blanche Romney—she had gone with Charles.

Unfortunately Catherine had not taken into account that there were people other than her employer who were interested in her affairs. When Honorine Cameron had observed Catherine's exit onto the darkened balcony with Lord Charles Musgrave, she had made her way to her nephew.

"And, by the by, Adam," she began after inviting him to an open house, the ostensible reason for their conversation, "I have always heard one should be especially careful of one's good friends. They often share one's tastes, or so it is said. Oh, I am only teasing. You needn't look so thunderous. I know Musgrave means nothing by leading Catherine onto the balcony; manners are so different today. In my day being alone with a gentleman was considered fast, but people are so much more broad-minded today, don't you think?"

To Honorine's disappointment, Clarendon's reply was neutral. Either her nephew was losing interest in his little betrothed or he had unlimited confidence in her loyalty. Unable to decide which as the case, Honorine left her nephew a frustrated woman.

Had she been more patient or more observant, the duke's aunt need not have felt so thwarted. Had she continued to watch him closely after their little chat, she'd have been treated to the sight of the duke maneuvering his dance partner in such a way that he kept the balcony entrance in view at all times. And, had she been so devoted as to keep her eye on her nephew throughout the long dance, she could have been treated to the ominous tightening of his jaw when he observed Catherine being escorted from the balcony by Charles, a satisfied smile curving her soft, full mouth.

21

*H*earing the sound of horses' hooves, Lady Anne looked ahead with quickened interest in her eyes. Her hopes were rewarded when in no more than a heartbeat, Lord Charles Musgrave appeared from around a curve in the path.

So pleased to see each other were the two lovers that only Catherine and young Jem, Catherine's groom, realized that the pounding of a horse's hooves could still be heard coming from behind them.

"Anne!" she called out in warning, fearful they would see Lynsford appear at any moment. To her astonishment, however, it was not the marquess who thundered around the long curve of trees by which she had just traveled. It was instead the tall, lean figure of her employer.

"Adam!" It was Charles, the last to see him, who spoke first.

"Charles," responded the duke, his voice cold enough to freeze, if his eyes, which were fastened on Catherine, had not already done so.

As the riders silently regarded one another, the horses stamped impatiently at the ground, snorting their displeasure with the tense stillness. The riders pulled at their reins, arranging themselves in a rough circle, with the duke set apart on one side and the other three riders drawn close together as if for protection. The duke's hooded gaze whipped over each of the others in turn. Only Catherine returned his furious regard, her chin raised defiantly.

"Why is it, I wonder, that I feel distinctly unwelcome in this cozy little group?" The duke's scornful voice broke the silence.

Catherine could see Anne's hands begin to tremble at the anger held only thinly in check in the duke's voice. Next to Anne, Charles' gelding pranced nervously. Poor Charles, she could see his brain working furiously to create a plausible explanation.

"Oh, have done, Adam," Catherine exclaimed, exasperated by the absurdity of the situation. "Obviously you have found out somehow that Anne and I meet a gentleman on our rides. Now you know that someone is Charles, and I doubt you've suffered a terrible surprise."

Surprise did flicker momentarily in the duke's hard eyes. He had expected angry denials when he confronted her, not weary exasperation. A completely new possibility occurred to him. It was, he saw, not Catherine who looked guilty, but Anne; not Catherine whose eyes strayed with fright to Charles, but Anne's.

Charles was looking from Catherine to the duke, observing the defiant set of her chin and the grim look in his friend's eye.

"Good Lord!" Charles' exclamation turned all eyes to him. "You think I've been meeting Catherine!" Without giving the duke a moment to respond, he turned apologetic eyes to Catherine. "I say, Catherine, I am sorry! I had no idea our affair might rebound on you like this."

"Think nothing of it, Charles." Catherine's voice was as stiff as her spine. "Believe me when I say it really matters very little what Clarendon thinks."

"But of course it matters, Catherine. The duke is your betrothed." This time it was Lady Anne who exclaimed in her soft voice.

"Perhaps we might make some progress if I were addressed directly." Adam's words were addressed to the group, but his glance, more thoughtful than before, lingered on Catherine.

"I can scarcely credit that you could think such a thing of Catherine, Adam." Charles fixed his friend with an accusing glare, which almost immediately turned into an affectionate grin. "Well, I suppose when one is in love, there is no saying what fancy your heart might believe. And I own these chance meetings may look compromising." Nodding his blond head toward Jem to remind his companions that there were other ears present, Charles added, "Come along to the lake, Adam, where we can be comfortable as well as private."

Catherine risked glancing at her employer as he came to help her dismount, and she was taken aback to see a distinctly triumphant gleam in his eye. It provoked her. How could he look as if he had just won a victory when he had been proven completely in the wrong?

When the two girls were seated on a little bench by the lake, Charles explained to his friend the circumstances of his relationship with Anne. The only untruth he told was to name the plan for meeting in the park under Catherine's cover, his own, but Catherine interrupted him, refusing to allow Charles to take the blame for her scheme. Her eyes sparkling with challenge, she had informed the duke that it was her idea and that she did not regret her action in the least.

The duke observed her flashing eyes and lifted chin a moment, but turned to Charles when he spoke. "I am, to say the least, quite surprised by your revelations, Charles. I never suspected there was anything between the two of you." He bowed to Anne, whose hazel eyes were filled with anxiety, and smiled reassuringly. "Rest assured, both of you, that I shall not say a word of what I have learned here this morning."

Anne's shoulders sagged a little with relief, and she returned the duke's smile. In a soft voice she thanked him while Charles did so more heartily.

"And you are certain Lynsford's objection is that you do not have adequate resources, Charles?" the duke asked after a moment.

"Afraid so, Adam," Charles answered. "At least that's what he told me and also told Anne. He wants to return the Lynsfords to their original glory and needs more than I have to do so."

Catherine was surprised to see the duke look at Anne with the most compassionate of expressions. "I hope you will believe that I sympathize with your plight, Lady Anne. Charles is a rascal"—he threw an amused look at his friend—"but he's a good rascal, for all that. However," he continued, his expression more serious, "you must understand I cannot allow Catherine to be involved in this affair any longer. I have the distinct notion that Lynsford can be quite nasty when challenged. I beg your pardon, Lady Anne, for putting it so plainly, but there it is. My first interest must be Catherine's well-being."

"And rightly so," Anne replied before anyone else could speak. "You are correct in your judgment of my brother, your grace. I have been utterly selfish to allow Catherine to become involved when she has no real idea of the consequences."

Anne turned urgently to her friend when Catherine made to protest. "No, Catherine, my dear, his grace is quite correct. Believe me, I have seen Lynsford aroused, and he can be a beast. I know it seems farfetched to you, but I believe it possible he could do you some harm for crossing him in this way. I would never forgive myself if something should happen to you. I have known all along we must stop treating him lightly, I just found it quite impossible to do so."

When Anne began to weep softly, Charles, throwing a disturbed glance at his friends, drew her away to comfort her in private.

Their departure left Catherine alone with the duke, and not pleased to be so. She suspected he would be very angry with her for having become embroiled in other peoples' affairs. And because she could not be so regretful of what she had done, she thought it likely a quarrel would ensue.

With uncharacteristic cowardice Catherine left him to walk down to the lake. She had brought, as she always did, some bread crumbs for the ducks, and a little flotilla of the birds swam silently toward her when she knelt by the edge of the water.

As she fed them, her thoughts remained on the man behind her. He had looked magnificent astride his dark stallion, his lean body taut as a whipcord, controlling the mettlesome animal with his customary ease. No! She violently flung out a crumb. She must not have such thoughts when she needed to keep a tight rein on her feelings.

"They seem to know you." The duke's voice startled her, but Catherine did not raise her eyes to his.

"I feed them every time I come. I suppose they've become accustomed to it," she explained, throwing a large piece to one of her favorites.

A silence fell again, and Catherine was nervously aware of the duke standing beside her, his eyes upon her as she tossed out the last of her tidbits. There could be no delaying the inevitable any longer, she thought, standing. It would be best to have the thing over and done, anyway. Tossing her head, Catherine flashed the duke a speaking look.

"Well? Aren't you going to upbraid me for being a fool, for involving myself in a situation of no concern to you, my employer?"

"Actually, I was thinking how the morning sun becomes you. Did you know your hair sometimes looks as if it had been touched by fire?" her employer drawled, a smile lurking in his gray eyes.

Catherine's face reflected the confusion his most unexpected words had thrown her into.

"At a loss for words, Catherine?" he asked in the same maddeningly amused tone. "That is hard to believe, and you know in polite company you are supposed to thank a gentleman when he pays you a compliment. Which I have just done, but if you missed it, what I said was you are very, very beautiful."

"You are trying to play me for a fool!" Catherine flushed at his praise, though she did not really believe he meant a word of it.

"I am not such a nodcock as to play you for a fool, Catherine. You are far too intelligent for that. All I am doing is trying to win your good side by telling you only what is true so that you will forgive me the unjust suspicions with which I have belabored you."

The look in the duke's eyes caused Catherine to take a deep breath and to turn quickly to look at the much-less-intense and much-less-demanding waters of the lake.

"You are not angry, then?" she asked softly.

"How could I be?" The duke's lean hand captured her chin, forcing her amber eyes to look up. His hand did not leave her chin immediately, but caressed it gently a moment while he looked searchingly at her.

Catherine could feel her knees begin to quiver and found it nearly impossible to return his look.

"Why did you not tell me?" he asked at last.

"Would you have believed me?" Catherine asked in her turn, her mouth twisting in a fleeting, bitter expression.

The duke, seeing it, released her chin and placed his finger on her lips as if to erase that testament to his injustice. "I might have believed you, I don't know," he said quietly, his eyes never leaving hers. "I wasn't given the chance to know."

Catherine's long dark lashes veiled her eyes. If she continued looking into that handsome face, which was regarding her with an unprecedented tenderness, she was afraid her own eyes would reveal all of her feelings to him. With an effort she forced her strangely sluggish mind to answer him.

"You forget that Charles asked me not to tell anyone, even you," she said, her voice not quite steady and only a little above a whisper.

"And you were willing to accept my accusations regarding Charles without thinking to tell Charles what a bee's nest his affairs had landed you in?"

There was a faint exasperation in the duke's tone that restored Catherine's equilibrium. After all, his lurid imagination was not her fault. He seemed to be accusing her of creating the "bee's nest" when anyone could see it had all been his doing. Her lashes raised as she shot him a hot look.

"If you had not thought it was Charles I had chosen as my catch, then I felt sure you would have imagined it to be another. I could not see that it would make a great deal of difference."

"I suppose I deserved that." The duke winced, raking his hand through his hair. Catherine had to remind herself to breathe as she watched a rueful smile play on his dark face. "I started out to beg your pardon, Catherine, not to upbraid you for keeping a trust. I feel a cad for all I've put you through."

"Not the Duke of Clarendon." Catherine tried for a light, chiding tone, but her voice was too gentle. She thought it would be best if she could look away from him, but she was powerless to do so. Something in his eyes made her heart pound so heavily it hurt.

"Will you forgive me, Catherine?" His voice was so low it enveloped her in a warm, intimate cocoon.

With a tremendous effort Catherine tried to shake off the strange feeling she had, as if she had fallen under a spell.

"Yes, I forgive you, your grace," she said after a long second of breathless silence. "I forgive you, that is, if you promise not to judge me so unfairly in the future."

"A just condition," allowed the duke, his eyes falling to Catherine's mouth.

Seeing the direction of his gaze, Catherine could scarcely think of anything save his mouth, which suddenly seemed very, very close. The responsible part of her mind tried to remind her of Lady Blanche and her new pendant. It tried to tell her that the duke could only be playing with her, that it was Lady Blanche he loved.

But Catherine did not listen to the warnings, for she was now far too absorbed with watching the duke's mouth descend to hers. His lips touched hers softly. When he withdrew, Catherine's lips ached for more.

Her cheeks burned scarlet when she realized her head was still turned, as if inviting the duke to another taste.

"Your grace," she implored, jerking her head down.

He chuckled softly then, and hearing it, Catherine flushed once again, this time with annoyance.

"Well! It may amuse you, but I am not accustomed to having kisses stolen," she informed him.

"Stolen?" the infuriating man had the gall to ask with an infuriating laugh lacing his low voice.

"Oh!" She glared at him, but the look in his hooded eyes drove all thought of anger from her mind. There was some amusement there, but there was more of something else, something that she could not exactly name, but that gleamed hot and dangerous.

For a very long moment, Catherine was held utterly spellbound by that look, aware only of it and the blood pounding through her veins. To her immense relief, it was then that Anne and Charles chose to reappear, their grave faces quenching, for the time being, the strange, almost helpless sensation the duke's scorching look had caused in her.

The trip home passed with little incident, Anne's depressed spirits keeping them all quiet on the first leg, and the concentration needed to maneuver high-spirited mounts in dense traffic taking care of the second. But when they had passed the tangle created by a driver who had misjudged the distance between his vehicle and a phaeton traveling in the opposite direction, the duke pulled his stallion close to Penelope. "Catherine," he said in a low, velvety voice that sent a thrill of alarm, as well as pleasure, through her. "I wonder why after all this time my given name seldom comes easily from you."

Catherine looked warily at her employer before she answered, her voice taking on the prim tone a schoolmistress might have used with a recalcitrant pupil. "I use your given name when it is correct to do so. You are my employer, and when there is no one else about, I cannot believe it is proper for me to take advantage of my role to presume familiarity."

"But surely there is no presumption where familiarity is desired, even requested," her employer persisted in an exceedingly innocent voice.

"To be sure," Catherine admitted in a neutral tone, immensely glad to see they had arrived at home. She had, as he perceived, avoided using Adam unless her part called for it, as there was something disturbingly intimate about addressing him by his given name. After her reaction to his advances in the park, she did not think now was the time to change her mind, but she would not draw attention to her discomfort by arguing the point. Instead, she would

escape into the house and allow the issue to lapse
naturally.

When the duke came to lift her down from Penelope's back, however, Catherine could detect a wicked
gleam in his eye, and she knew the issue would not
be allowed to fade away, after all.

"Please, Adam?" He grinned, his hands holding
her waist but not lifting her.

His charm was nearly tangible, and Catherine had
to force herself not to smile besottedly. "Please, Adam,"
she repeated, using all her acting skills to make her
voice playful. There was only the heightened color
in her cheeks to betray to the careful observer how
disconcerting the concession had been.

22

*I*n the early afternoon, after luncheon, if they had no other engagements, Lady de Maine and Catherine often met to chat companionably in Lady de Maine's private sitting room. A charming jonquil-colored room, it served as Lady de Maine's special sanctum, to be entered only by invitation. Having long since won a permanent place in Lady de Maine's affections, Catherine could enter at will, but the consideration that made her so dear to Lady de Maine bade her this afternoon, as every other afternoon, to knock before she entered.

Delighted to see her, Lady de Maine waved her to a seat and resumed the needlework she had been busy with when Catherine knocked.

Catherine, too, took up a piece of embroidery that she had left in a basket set aside for that purpose. The two women had been chatting only a few moments when Catherine emitted an unladylike squeal.

"Drat!" She winced, sucking the drop of blood from her pricked finger.

"You did not spend an excessive amount of your childhood with a needle in hand, did you, child?" Lady de Maine asked, a smile in her gray eyes.

"Not an excessive amount, no," Catherine admitted with a grin. "Most of my time I spent on horseback or with a book, I am afraid. Shall I ever get the hang of this, do you think, Aunt Emily?"

Lady de Maine's eyes fell to the sampler in Catherine's lap. The stitches on it were uneven and their placement was irregular. Obviously at a loss for a polite answer, Lady de Maine looked hesitantly at her companion only to find Catherine's amber eyes dancing with golden sparks of amusement.

"You are funning me, miss," Lady de Maine scolded, laughing. "I know that mischievous grin."

Her grin turned down a trifle as Catherine surveyed her work. "Well, I am sure it would be difficult to find a more poorly executed sampler than this one. Nor do I believe I shall continue tormenting myself. My fingers are cramped and bloody after their campaign."

"In that case my dear, I wonder if I might ask a favor of you?"

When Catherine readily agreed, Lady de Maine asked her to run an errand in Bond Street. "I should like some more blue ribbon for the headpiece I shall wear tomorrow to Freddy's affair at Vauxhall. Unfortunately I cannot go myself, as I have an appointment at Suzette's. Nor do I fancy sending Gadsen, poor thing. Her eyesight is failing, you know. The last time I asked her to match ribbon, it was a perfect disaster, but I had to wear it anyway for fear of hurting her feelings."

Laughing at Lady de Maine's mock horror, Catherine said she would be delighted to go.

Accordingly, some few moments later, Catherine, accompanied by Peg, was seated in the Clarendon carriage. Normally, when the two girls were together, they chattered amicably about the latest event Catherine had attended, as Peg had developed an appetite for the doings of the quality, but today the carriage was quiet while Catherine stared out the window, obviously distracted.

She was thinking about the evening before, but she was not at all ready to discuss it. She recalled with a sigh how nervous she had been descending the stairs, dressed in a silver gauze gown, a soft white silk shawl draped about her shoulders. She'd not seen Clarendon since he had lifted her from Penelope's back after the park, and she had felt a knot in her stomach at the thought of facing him. It seemed more than likely that a man of the duke's experience must know how he affected her, and she shrank from meeting his knowing eyes. But she need not have worried. As if he had determined he would bring her only pleasure, the duke had treated her from the start of the evening to its end with a tender, thrilling courtesy. Not once had he made her blush, nor had he even once regarded her with that sardonic lift of his brows that could chill her so thoroughly. His eyes had followed her, but his eyes had been lit with pleasure as he watched her twirl by him. Her spirits had soared when he claimed the first waltz, but when he had come to claim a second, an unnatural shyness had overcome her. Suddenly it seemed their relationship had reached a new stage, and she was not sure what her role was, nor even what she wanted it to be. After several moments of feeling stiff and unnatural, intensely aware of his arm encircling her waist, Catherine had subdued her cautioning voice. She would treat herself to the pleasure of his arms around her and worry what it all meant later.

In the morning light on her way to Bond Street, she was worrying what it all meant. Today she remembered Blanche's pendant, remembered the duke only knew her as an actress, remembered how only recently her employer had firmly believed her to be a low schemer. It did not seem likely that the duke's intentions toward her could be honorable. A pain stabbed her breast at the thought, and she found herself close to wishing she had never met the Duke of Clarendon.

"We're here, miss." Peg's cheery voice prevented her from coming to any resolution.

Her gloom dissipated a little as she strolled down the busy street, nodding to several acquaintances out on errands of their own before entering the little shop that sold ribbon. Mr. Bobbins, the shopkeeper, recognized her and bustled about to accommodate her. With three samples in her hand she stepped to the window, idly glancing out as she did so. The sight that met her eyes was so totally unexpected and so totally horrible, the blood left her cheeks. There, looking about frantically, stood someone she had all but forgotten, her guardian, Rudolph Spenser. How he came to be in London on Bond Street before the very store she had entered, Catherine did not know, but some sixth sense warned her that his darting eyes were looking for her. He was standing back from the shops, as if trying to keep his eye on several doors at once, and if she had not seen him first, she would have walked straight into his arms. The thought sent a fresh wave of horror through her.

Pulling herself together after a few moments, Catherine selected the correct shade of ribbon and then asked the shopkeeper if he would be so good as to indulge a whim of hers. Catherine explained she had just seen pass by a gentleman who had the most annoying *tendre* for her. Her lashes fluttering sweetly, Catherine gave Mr. Bobbins the distinct impression that he could perform the most extraordinary service for her if he would only allow her to leave by his back door. Only too eager to please the future Duchess of Clarendon—and her such a beautiful, sweet lady as well—Mr. Bobbins personally escorted her and Peg out the back and down the service alley. They reached the carriage without incident, though Catherine, breathing a sigh of relief, took the precaution of keeping her face well away from the window.

She would not have been nearly so relieved had she known that Rudolph's sharp eyes had picked her out when she left the alleyway. He had not gotten a good look at the crest on the carriage she had entered, but he had gotten a look at the matched bays pulling it and knew he would be able to find the fancy rig eventually. It seemed he had been wise to come to London in search of his treacherous ward. Judging from her dress and the carriage, she looked to have landed on her feet, and he intended to collect in full what she owed him for the loss of Hugo Overstreet and for the embarrassment he had suffered.

Catherine, as she rode back home, guessed at least the last part of her cousin's thoughts. Her earlier worries about the duke and his intentions seemed nothing next to her anxiety about what Rudolph would do if he found her. Whatever she did, she must not fall into Rudolph's greedy, malevolent clutches again. It was cowardly, she knew, but more than anything, she wanted to stay at home this night. Perhaps by the morrow she would have rallied her spirits enough to venture out again, but tonight she wanted to stay behind the protective walls of Clarendon House.

Therefore, Lady de Maine's first words to her, after she had gratefully accepted the ribbon, were most welcome.

"You've just missed Adam, my dear," the duke's aunt informed her. "He said to make an excuse to you about this evening. Said he was off with a Mr. Brown. He didn't say why or where, but he assured me you would understand."

Aunt Emily's gray eyes regarded Catherine quizzically, but she avoided the questions so plainly written in them. "Ah," Catherine explained, "Mr. Brown is an associate of Adam's."

Lady de Maine cast her a shrewd glance. "That's

as namby-pamby an answer as Adam's was. An associate in what, I might ask, but I can tell from the look on your pretty face, you would be distressed if I did. Which leaves me to wonder just why you would be distressed. But there, my dear, you look a bit peaked and I shall resist teasing you anymore."

This gave Catherine the opening to say she had in fact developed a headache, and if Aunt Emily did not object, she would cry off the evening's card party at the Wyndham's. On the instant Lady de Maine whisked Catherine to her room, where she commanded her to stay.

"I've let you wear yourself to a frazzle. I declare your megrim is a result of fatigue, and that condition is entirely my fault," she clucked sympathetically.

Catherine, smiling wanly, admonished her not to blame herself, but remained in the bed, glad to shut out Rudolph in its cozy depths.

23

Catherine did fall asleep, but her nap brought her little rest. Rudolph, looming larger than life and more threatening, lurked in wait for her each time she had closed her eyes. When Lady de Maine departed for the Wyndham's, Catherine gave up pretending to have a headache and escaped her room to seek out some diversion.

Clad only in a dressing gown of soft lawn, her thick, dark hair flowing loosely down her back, Catherine made her way through the quiet house to the duke's library. It had been in the library at her home that she had often found refuge as a child, and the duke's wood-paneled room, though larger, gave her much the same feeling of comfort. A fire had been lit, and its light bathed the room in a warm, coppery glow.

Catherine breathed deeply, inhaling the reassuringly familiar smells of the polish and the fire, and smiled slightly as she felt the knot of tension in her stomach uncoil. Running an appreciative eye over the stacks upon stacks of books, their leather bindings gleaming in the firelight, she selected a volume, and hoping its content could keep her distracted, she adjourned to the couch.

It was there in his library that some hours later the duke, having returned from his business, found her.

His business with Mr. Brown had been concluded with more success than he had dared to hope. They had been able to follow the man with the crescent-shaped scar to a not unfamiliar house. His brother's murderer was identified. All that was left to do was to marshal his evidence against the villain.

To celebrate his victory and to bury bitter thoughts of Gerald, for whom the victory was too late, the duke had stopped by his club. As he had hoped, Freddy was there, ready and willing to match him drink for drink.

When Clarendon, who, though not in his cups, was still feeling no pain, found his employee curled like a kitten on his couch, her magnificent hair spreading like a dark, fiery cloud around her, a book—by Molière, he found on examination—lying on the floor beside her, and her breast rising gently against the soft, thin fabric of her gown, he was in no frame of mind to resist the impulse to further celebrate his success in her embrace.

Feeling something brush her cheek, Catherine fluttered her eyes open. The deep sleep into which she had at last fallen still clinging to her mind, she was not certain she was not dreaming, but with a thrill of pleasure, she thought it was the duke's handsome face she saw above her. And he was smiling at her too, she thought dreamily to herself, smiling in return.

She struggled to sit up, unaware of the seductive picture her thin dressing gown made as it outlined her figure, and because the fire had died down, she shivered.

"You mustn't take a chill," the duke scolded her when he felt her body quiver. He sounded so like a nursemaid that Catherine giggled. "Laugh all you like." He grinned down at her, making her heart lurch and at the same time scooping her into his arms. "We mustn't have you taking cold. I cannot have people saying I do not take care of you as you deserve."

Before she could even think to utter any protest, if

indeed she had had any intention of doing so, the duke carried her to a chair closer to the fire and sat her down in his lap.

"We shall tuck your feet in here, your head should rest here on my shoulder, and I shall chafe warmth back into your hands," he said, still playing the role of nanny.

Catherine knew she was not dreaming, and she knew quite well that she should protest their intimate position. It was a thought she had no trouble whatsoever ignoring. With all her being Catherine desired to remain exactly where she was.

Her sudden lack of restraint did not owe a great deal to her sleepy, dreamlike feeling, though that did help. It was her meeting with Rudolph that kept her in the duke's arms. Seeing him had made her feel alone, unprotected, and very vulnerable.

But in the duke's strong arms those feelings were held at bay. Here she was secure, as if she were in a magic circle. In this enchanted place, her wicked guardian could not threaten her.

"How fortunate I am to find such a lovely kitten asleep on my couch. Should I flatter myself that you chose to await my return at home rather than enjoy the attentions of the *ton*, or is there some other reason you have missed your evening's engagement?"

The duke's deep, lazy voice, whispering into her ear, sent a shiver of excitement through her. From the folds of his cravat, Catherine gave a contented sigh. "I confess I stayed home on my own account. I needed a rest."

"You are well, though?" The duke's hand tipped up her chin, and Catherine's heart skipped a beat at the real concern in her eyes.

"I am fine," she whispered breathlessly, aware that his eyes were a smoky color she had never seen before.

Slowly, so slowly it seemed time had been altered,

the duke's mouth descended to hers. She never once thought of avoiding it, she watched its descent as if mesmerized. When his lips met hers, she heard a groan and realized it came from her. Twice before he had kissed her, once angrily, once lightly, but this time was what she had unconsciously been waiting for. Gentle at first, the kiss became, as she responded to it, more passionate, its hot promise thrilling her.

At this point, the Duke of Clarendon, sophisticated, experienced man of the world, made an irretrievable mistake. Normally he would have pressed his advantage and made the lady his. But tonight, perhaps because he suddenly remembered that, having discovered his enemy's identity, he had no reason to keep Catherine with him; or perhaps because the sweet urgency of Catherine's untutored response thrilled him as nothing ever had, he lingered a moment. Tenderly, he pushed Catherine's tumbled hair back from her face and with one long finger outlined her soft, reddened lips.

"It seems I have waited a long time for this, my sweet," he whispered, his lazy voice husky. "You are incomparably beautiful, you know. It's been hell to keep my hands off you even when I thought the worst of you. That's why I took such pains never to be alone with you, but now we'll make up for that. You'll stay with me, and there will be no more theater or dingy little boarding rooms. I'll keep you in a splendid little house in Albemarle Street where you'll have lovely jewels and all the silks and satins you want."

Slowly, against her will, Catherine's mind began to register his words. He was asking her—no, assuming she would be his mistress. Mistress! The word contended for her attention with the feel of his mouth raining kisses on her eyes.

"Amethysts, I think," he stopped again. "Though even they will not do justice to your eyes."

The words kept coming, kept intruding, and try as she might to forget them, they only echoed more loudly in her mind. He would buy her, they seemed to say, for his use. She would give to him all she had, and he, in return, would give her amethysts to match her eyes. Just as a sapphire pendant had matched the eyes of his other mistress. That unexpected thought, like a bucket of ice water, sobered her completely.

With a sob, she sprang away from him, landing on the floor a few feet from him in a crouch, her amber eyes still heavy with desire, her breast heaving, though whether from desire or anger even she could not have said.

Not in the least expecting her to flee, the duke made no move to stop her. His lap felt cold where she had been, and for a long moment he merely stared blankly at the figure crouching before him.

"What the hell are you doing?" he asked at last in a voice that held more surprise than anger.

Catherine regarded him silently for a long moment, achingly aware that she still desired him; then, remembering his words, she said simply, "I cannot be your doxy, your grace."

As her words penetrated the fog desire had created in his mind, Catherine watched the color of his eyes change from the smoky gray that had so fascinated her to the icy silver that could so intimidate her.

Uncoiling himself from his chair, he towered over her as she knelt on the floor. "What in the hell do you mean? You want me, you know you do. Of course you will be my mistress!"

His arrogance sparked Catherine's temper as much now as it ever had. "Do you plan to tie me up, your grace?" she spat at him, her eyes flashing gold sparks. "For that is the only way I shall be your mistress, unwillingly."

His eyes lit with a frightening, angry fire when he heard her intemperate words. Jerking her to her feet, he shook her shoulders and demanded in a voice tight with fury, "What is this game you are playing now? It's a dangerous one, I warn you, Catherine. Is it that you want something I haven't offered? A better address than Albemarle Street perhaps, or diamonds rather than amethysts?"

Catherine blinked back angry tears. His words made it very clear what sort of person he thought her. "No, there is nothing more I want," she said in a small voice. "I only want to be left alone."

Her statement was not exactly the truth. Even now, with his body close to hers again, she longed to fall into his arms, to accept any terms he offered. It was only by drawing on every ounce of strength she had that she was able to deny him with a steady, unwavering stare.

The duke looked hard at the disheveled beauty before him, almost unable to believe she had changed from the passionate, sensuous woman of only moments ago to this angry, stubborn vixen. He did not know what her intent was, but seeing the implacable look in her eyes, he was overwhelmed by anger. Releasing her with a curse, he said with icy disdain, "Go then, mistress, it shall be as you please. But know this when you do, the most disgusting of all women is the tease, the vixen who promises much but withdraws the fulfillment of her promise for some reason, some game of her own. Whatever you had hoped to gain with this . . . this performance, you have lost. I only want you out of my sight."

Irresolute, torn by her own conflicting feelings, Catherine watched with horror as a flat disgust for her filled his eyes. She had not meant to lead him on, had not known what she was doing as she responded to his touch. She wanted to catch his hand, to beg his pardon, to tell him her circumstances, to say that she loved him, to say that she would be his lover, but not his mistress.

"Go!" he roared suddenly, pushing her toward the door. "Can't you even hear? You are either a fool or a vixen, and I will not abide either one."

Unable to explain, knowing he would never understand, nor trust her again, Catherine fled the room, running all the way to her own.

24

"Ah, there you are, Catherine," Lady de Maine's voice hailed Catherine as she descended the stairs. "My dear, you look even more lovely than usual. Suzette was right to say this clinging style is perfect for a figure like yours."

Catherine smiled her thanks at Lady de Maine even as her eyes sought the reaction of the person standing behind her. Nervously, her eyes flickered to the Duke of Clarendon, looking rakishly handsome as ever in his dark evening clothes. In an instant the hope of reconciliation, which she had nursed all day, died. With a sick feeling, she saw his hooded gray eyes turn upon her without the least response reflected there. For all the interest he showed, she might have been a serving girl come to bring his aunt's wrap. There was not even a word of greeting, only a slight bow, which Catherine guessed he felt forced by his aunt's presence to accord her.

Nor was the carriage ride to Vauxhall Gardens any more comfortable. Seated beside the duke, his broad shoulders so near to her that the warmth of his body and the scent of his cologne vividly recalled their tryst the night before, Catherine could almost feel his disinterest in her. He responded occasionally to Lady de Maine's light chatter, but for the most part kept his head turned to look out the window, ignoring completely the woman at his side. Only once, when the carriage lurched into a rut and threw her against him, did Catherine gain his attention. But the sudden, rigid tension she felt in the muscles beneath her hand proved to her that he could not abide even her inadvertent touch.

At Vauxhall, the duke left her immediately after escorting her to the bandstand area where Freddy was holding his party. The setting was a lovely one, the tiny lights of the lanterns hanging in the trees creating a magical fairyland out of the gardens, but Catherine only noticed that Lady Blanche was in the group the duke joined.

It was not the last of his attentions to that lady. When he led Blanche onto the floor for the third time, Catherine could feel the speculative eyes fixed on her as she danced, and she fancifully imagined she could hear the whisperings passed along behind their fans as the dowagers gossiped knowingly on this unexpected turn of events.

It was a measure of her tension that when Eustace appeared, Catherine was relieved to accept his invitation for a stroll. She wanted only to escape the painful sight of the man who had wanted to make her his mistress, flaunting his preference for the woman he had wanted to make his wife.

Catherine and Eustace walked for some time, Eustace chattering all the while, though Catherine could not have named the subject, when he asked if she would mind sitting awhile. Seeing that he was out of breath, Catherine readily agreed and sat quietly breathing in the cool night air.

So lost was she in her temporary peace that it took a few moments to recognize the murmuring voice she heard in the background. Finally, however, recognition dawned. Somewhere close at hand, but screened by hedges, the Duke of Clarendon was speaking in a low, intimate voice to another person.

"I am awaiting the reward due me for following

you so obligingly." Catherine heard him chuckle, then there was silence.

The silence was eventually broken by the throaty sound of Blanche Romney's voice. "I have missed you, Adam. No one can thrill me as you do, but I feared you had decided to let your young bride keep us apart."

"She has nothing to do with us," he replied, his voice cool, then added in a more drawling voice, "No, not here. Come away to a quieter place where we need not fear any interruption."

Until their departure, Catherine had been held frozen in her place, but as their footsteps receded, her mind began to function once again.

"I say, Miss Asterley, I did not know . . ." Eustace's voice, laden with false sympathy, faded away at the look he saw in Catherine's eyes.

"Don't bother to lie, Eustace." Catherine's voice was hoarse with her anger as she leaned over him. "You have enough sins on your head, there is no reason to add lying to them. You are a disgusting, scheming toad. Adam may prefer Blanche, as you and your mother have both gone to great pains to demonstrate, but he will not be pleased to learn you have tried to use his private affairs for your own gain. And make no mistake, Eustace, he shall know."

Hurrying back to find Lady de Maine so that she might plead illness and leave the party entirely, Catherine tried to console herself with the thought that at least her work for the duke was completed. Indolent appearances to the contrary, Eustace must be the villain who had plotted to kill Gerald and now plotted against the duke. No one else had tried to prevent her supposed marriage. Only Eustace and his mother had attempted to do so . . . and Lady Blanche, of course, but her motives were obvious.

"Miss Asterley?" the Marquess of Lynsford's voice halted her headlong rush. "Sorry to startle you, but I thought you might be in need of assistance. It is not at all safe, you know, to be in the gardens alone. May I be of service?"

Looking about, Catherine realized she could no longer see the bright lights of the area around the bandstand and would need the marquess if she was to return safely. Taking his arm gratefully, she explained only that she had had cause to leave her escort and had lost her way.

"Such an easy thing to do, here." The marquess smiled.

After they had walked for several moments, it occurred to Catherine that now she could not even hear the noise of the party. If anything, this area was more deserted than that where the marquess had joined her.

"Where are we going, my lord?" she demanded, frowning. "This does not seem to be the way back, after all. I wish to be taken to Lady de Maine."

"I am afraid, my dear, that is not possible," her escort said, a frightening, gloating note in his voice. "You see, you are going with me."

Truly afraid now, Catherine turned to run, but before she could go very far, a great blow struck her head and she felt nothing more.

25

"Freddy, have you seen Catherine or Adam? I am afraid I've lost sight of them both for some time."

Lady de Maine's face as she looked at Freddy reflected concern and a little guilt as well. Diverted by the latest *on-dits* with which Mrs. Jarred had been regaling her, she had forgotten to keep a friendly eye on Catherine. Now she did not see her anywhere, nor could she find her nephew to inquire if Catherine was with him.

"I believe I saw Catherine go for a walk with Eustace, Aunt Em," Freddy told her. "As for Adam, well, I cannot say exactly where he's got to."

Lady de Maine looked closely at Freddy, whose eyes seemed to be avoiding hers. "Do you mean, Freddy, that Adam has gone for a walk with someone else? Blanche Romney, no doubt. I vow I shall never know what he sees in that mercenary harpy."

"No more do I, Aunt Emily," muttered Freddy under his breath. "Ah, look! I believe I see Adam now."

Freddy did not add, though he could not have avoided seeing, that the duke was returning from the gardens with a tellingly disheveled Lady Blanche.

Lady de Maine beckoned to her nephew, who, after a few words to Lady Blanche, joined her.

"Adam, I hope you can take your mind off that woman a moment?"

The duke arched an eyebrow at his aunt's unusually sarcastic tone. "If you need my assistance, Aunt Emily, I stand ready to serve you. If, however, you have called me to your side to ring a peal over me, then I shall be on my way."

Lady de Maine's hand prevented her nephew from turning away. "I cannot like her, Adam, I never have," she responded, looking directly into his cool eyes. "However, it is not of her I wish to ask you, but of Catherine. I fear I have lost sight of her for quite some time. Surely no harm will befall her among friends, but she does not know the gardens and I am somewhat concerned. Have you seen her?"

"I've not seen her since we arrived, but I am certain Catherine can take care of herself."

Lady de Maine and Freddy exchanged startled glances in response to the duke's indifferent tone. "Well, Adam may not wish to help for some unfathomable reason, Aunt Emily." Freddy cast a reproachful look at his friend. "But I do. I shall ask Eustace if he knows what has become of her."

Freddy had already started walking toward Eustace's bulky figure when he was brought up short by the duke's hand on his shoulder.

"What has Eustace to do with Catherine, Freddy?" he demanded, his eyes having lost the detached look of only a moment before.

"Why, Eustace was the last person I saw with Catherine," Freddy answered. "They went for a walk about the same time that you left with Blanche."

"Eustace took Catherine for a walk?" the duke repeated, frowning in the direction of his cousin. "I don't believe I've ever seen Eustace walk more than the distance to the refreshment table, have you, Freddy?" It was a rhetorical question to which the duke expected no answer, for he abruptly stalked past Freddy and, reaching Eustace, pulled him roughly aside.

"Aunt Emily informs me she has not seen Catherine for some time, Eustace, and Freddy reports you were the last person seen with her. You took her for a walk at the same time Blanche persuaded me to take a stroll with her, I understand. I wonder, Eustace, where you took Catherine for her walk, and why you do not seem to have returned with her."

Eustace swallowed convulsively, his neckcloth suddenly feeling quite tight. "We, we just went for a walk, Adam. She was tired of the crowd around her and needed a breath of air."

"How fortunate that you were so available, Eustace, but how unfortunate that you misplaced her. Tell me, is it possible she overheard a certain private conversation?"

Eustace wiped the drops of sweat that had popped out on his brow, wishing Blanche were here to answer. The idea was hers, really, hatched on the spur of the moment tonight when Clarendon seemed to be favoring her again, and he had only agreed to it when she had assured him she would be able to handle the duke.

Adam regarded the sweating face of his heir and needed no answer. "Yes, I see now," he drawled derisively. He turned to look at Blanche, who stood only a little distance away talking with some friends. Feeling eyes on her, she looked up, smiling coyly when she saw who it was that stared so. Her seductive smile faded, however, when she detected the hard look in his eyes, then vanished entirely when she took in the stricken look on Eustace's face. It was all the confirmation the duke needed.

"What happened to Catherine after she overheard Blanche and me, Eustace?" The duke's lock on his arm caused Eustace to stammer hurriedly that she had run away without him. "If any harm befalls Catherine because of you, Eustace, you will regret it," the duke promised his cousin in a deadly whisper before he left him.

"Freddy," Clarendon called as he surveyed the crowd intently, "Catherine left Eustace near that water fountain with all the cherubs. She is alone now, and we must find her quickly. Lynsford came tonight, did he not?"

"Yes, he's here." Freddy looked about. "Hmm, I don't see him just now, but he was here. Can't think what you want with him. I invited him only because of Anne, and she couldn't even come. He said she's taken ill."

"Never mind." The duke was walking away rapidly. "We must find Catherine as quickly as possible. Pray God we're not too late. We'll start looking where she left Eustace."

Half an hour later the two men met at the spot where they had parted, each with only failure to report. There was no sign of Catherine, nor, the duke noted with a thinning of his lips, was there any sign of the Marquess of Lynsford.

Deciding quickly, he told Freddy to continue discreetly searching the gardens with a groom for assistance while he left to look for Catherine at home.

With no explanation, he hurried Lady de Maine to the coach and commanded the coachman to make all haste to Clarendon House.

"But, Adam!" Lady de Maine protested. "What on earth are you doing? Why have we left? Where is Catherine?"

"I very much fear, Aunt Emily, she is in a carriage with Lord Lynsford heading I can only guess where."

"What?" she gasped, her voice quavering.

At the sight of her distress, the duke tore his mind from Catherine. "It's a long story, Aunt Emily. Suffice it to say for the time being that I believe Lynsford means Catherine harm, and through my own carelessness I may have allowed her to come into his grasp. It is possible, though, that she has left the party for another reason and returned home. We shall see in a moment. Please try to be patient until then."

After what seemed like hours to both the occupants of the carriage, Clarendon House came into view. Before the carriage had come to a full stop, the duke leapt down and, striding up the steps, opened the door of the mansion, shouting for Davies and Peg.

Davies arrived first and, having informed his master that Miss Asterley had not come home, was dispatched with orders to locate and fetch Mr. Thomas Brown, have Ares and another mount saddled, and organize food supplies for two pairs of saddlebags.

When Peg arrived a moment later, she confirmed Davies' report and added in reply to a barked question that, no, Miss Catherine had not been home and left again.

"Adam, will you tell me what is going on?" Lady de Maine pleaded when at last they were alone in the library.

The duke looked at his aunt, lines of care evident on his face. "I have a long confession to make, Aunt Emily. It is time you knew the whole."

In as few words as possible her nephew told her of his suspicions concerning his brother's death and of the scheme he had devised to force the murderer to show his hand. Looking away from his aunt, the duke informed her that his betrothed was, in fact, an actress, one Nancy Wright.

"I also hired a Mr. Brown to investigate any strangers who were around Clarendon Hall at the time of Gerald's death. Both of my employees served me well, for each in their way provided me with information that indicated the Marquess of Lynsford to be the man I've been seeking. Yes, it is a shocking thought, I know, but I have learned he had reason to hate the Camerons. It was my father who won the game in which the old marquess lost the last of his fortune. Apparently, Lynsford never got over the shock of the loss and has held a secret bitterness toward our family ever since. Now I fear Lynsford, having learned how close I was on his trail, has struck the first blow in our final battle and abducted Catherine to use as the bait with which to capture me."

Throughout her nephew's incredible story, Lady de Maine had sat quite still; only her gray eyes, as they searched his face, revealed the shock and worry she felt.

"I hardly know what to say, Adam." She shook her head when he had finished. "To learn suddenly that your betrothal was nothing but a hoax, that that dear, lovely girl is an actress, is outside of enough. But, then, to be told that the Marquess of Lynsford is a murderer who killed my nephew and is now trying to kill you . . . My dear, it strains the imagination."

"I know. Sometimes I've doubted the whole thing myself." There was an unusual air of apology in the duke's manner as he regarded his aunt. "And I know how wretched it must be to have had me play such a trick on you with Catherine. I did it only after a great deal of thought and with a great deal more reluctance. I believed it necessary if you were to act naturally with her. You will forgive me?"

"Oh, Adam, my dear boy, of course I do," Lady de Maine exclaimed as she looked at the tall, proud figure of her nephew. "I know how dearly you loved Gerald."

Adam saluted her with a kiss. "You are a champ, my love. And I hope you will help me now."

"How may I do so?" she asked, and her nephew bowed acknowledgment of her pluck.

"Put it about that Catherine took ill, that someone,

Lynsford perhaps, saw her home, and that she and I, both, will not be able to go out for a few days."

At his aunt's nod the duke flashed her a worried smile and kissed her cheek before leaving hurriedly to change into riding clothes.

As he rushed down the stairs, only a quarter of an hour later, Davies opened the door to admit a small, nondescript man.

"Brown! Come, follow me and I shall explain what's up." The duke continued out the door, Brown following in his wake. "Take the roan, Brown, we've a ride ahead of us."

After they had mounted and left the house, the duke turned to his confederate. "I believe Lynsford has abducted Miss Asterley tonight from Vauxhall Gardens. It is my guess he will make for his hunting box in Redford. It is more remote and secluded than his home and has the added advantage of having fewer servants about to say him nay. Do you agree?"

"Aye. I think that's likely. When did the abduction occur, your grace?" Mr. Brown's voice was as calm as if they discussed the weather.

"No more than two or three hours ago. He has a start on us, but he must be traveling by carriage. Catherine would not willingly go with him, and he would have to bind and gag her to prevent her setting up an alarm."

The two men fell silent as they concentrated on making their way through London as quickly as possible. As he maneuvered his mount expertly, the duke finally allowed himself to think of Catherine. He imagined her lying helpless before the man he believed to be capable of murder. At the thought an agony as intense as that he had experienced when he had learned of his brother's death, rocked him.

The duke felt for the pistols he had put in each pocket. He had all the more reason now to welcome the hour when he could claim his revenge on

Lynsford. Not only would the madman pay for Gerald, he would also answer for his abduction of Catherine.

At long last the city's crowds thinned, and the duke, with a savage snarl, urged Ares to a gallop.

26

Reluctantly Catherine became aware of a terrible pain throbbing in her head. She tried to lie perfectly still, then realized she was swaying because she was moving. Carriage wheels bounced into a rut, confirming her notion and sending a fresh wave of pain through her head. She tried to steady herself, then became aware she was bound at the hands and feet and had a gag in her mouth.

Firmly pushing terror and pain aside, Catherine tried to think. She could hear tree branches scraping the side of the carriage as if they were in a narrow lane, and the thought of trees recalled Vauxhall, then immediately the marquess. He had actually abducted her, Catherine's groggy mind struggled to accept the absurd idea.

Not many minutes later, the carriage rolled to a stop, and the door opened to reveal Lynsford holding a lantern in his raised hand.

"I see my little passenger has come around." Catherine could do nothing to wipe from his face the smile she could just make out in the dim light. "And none the worse for wear, I believe."

Setting the lantern aside, he lifted Catherine, carrying her into a small cottage, up a steep, narrow set of steps to the first of two small rooms that opened onto a small upper hallway.

There was no light here at all, so Catherine could only guess that the paler areas of the room, high above her, were windows. Her captor dropped her onto a rough, small bed, then reached down to withdraw the gag.

Catherine licked her dry lips and swallowed to soothe her miserably parched throat. "What do you want with me?" Her voice was a scarcely recognizable croak.

The marquess laughed a gloating, altogether chilling laugh as he lit a lantern that had been left in the bare little room. "I gave you the chance to come to me willingly, Miss Asterley, but you refused. I wasn't grand enough or wealthy enough. How do you feel about the grander Clarendon now? Still believe he will make the perfect husband? Oh, yes, I saw the scene with Blanche. I never thought Eustace could be so clever. I must remember to thank him; he made my little problem so much simpler."

"Whatever do you mean?" Catherine's mind, muddled by throbbing pain, was having difficulty grasping Lynsford's purpose. She could hear the excited anger in his voice, but the only thing she had done worthy of such anger was to aid Anne, and he had not mentioned his sister. And the duke . . . Her mind turned at last to him. Would he know what had happened? There had been no witnesses to her abduction. She had left the party with Eustace, not Lynsford. No, he could have no way of knowing what had happened to her, even if he cared enough to pursue them.

As if he had read her thoughts, Lynsford said, "Clarendon will come. He has suspected me for some time now. Did he think I wouldn't know if he sent someone to ask my servants questions? Ha! It served my purpose to allow him to suspect. He'll chase after us, he wants my head, and he won't want to lose you despite his silly games with Blanche. I've seen the way he looks at you. Ha! Ha! But I'll get you first. I'll tell him I've had you before I kill him."

This time the marquess's laughter sounded truly demonic. Staring in horror at his contorted face, Catherine understood his intent at last. The Marquess of Lynsford was the man they had sought. He was Gerald's murderer. Had Adam indeed suspected? she wondered frantically, the first ray of hope dawning.

"Why?" Catherine asked, the anguish she felt making her voice break.

"Why? Why do I want to kill the Duke of Clarendon as I did his brother? Yes, yes, I had his brother killed. So simple to string a thin wire across the path and snap his neck when he came along at a full gallop. Ha! Ha! I got the idea after his mother and father died so suddenly. God's justice for their sins! Come, come, why do you look so horrified? They deserved to die. It was the old duke who broke my father in a card game. He took my inheritance, but I'll have my revenge when I've killed his last son and married my sister to Eustace. Ha! What an heir! I've made it my business to learn all his unsavory little habits. There's a little opera dancer who was found dead, and I don't think Eustace will want it to get about who was responsible. You saw how green he turned just at my mention of the word 'opera,' didn't you? Ha! He'll go along, and settle a large sum on me as well."

'You'll never enjoy that money," Catherine spat weakly. "Too many people know about you."

"Quiet," the marquess screamed. He slapped her, and after a fresh, violent wave of pain rocked her, Catherine slumped onto the bed.

She awoke when the door was abruptly flung open. Lynsford entered, a cup in his hand and a heavy pistol tucked into the waistband of his breeches.

"There's no need to look so fearful, my lovely," he greeted her as she eyed the weapon. "I've brought some wine, and in a little while we shall have the food my good Will is preparing below."

A faint light was coming in the window, allowing Catherine to see the glitter of excitement shining in her assailant's pale eyes. A shiver of revulsion shook her.

"Shivering? We'll take care of that in no time, my love. You'll have desire to warm you very soon." The marquess's thin lips curled into a leer. "I have wanted you for such a long time. At first I thought I was only interested in you because you belonged to Clarendon, but then I realized that I desired you for your own sake. It was then I decided to have you one way or the other."

"Stop this nonsense and release me," Catherine demanded, anger overcoming her fear.

"Oh, come, come, Catherine," the marquess chided as if she had said something childish. He stood over her, tipping her head back to allow the wine to trickle into her mouth. When a drop rolled down her cheek, the marquess wiped it, then trailed his finger down her neck.

Bound and helpless, Catherine felt his hand slowly proceed downward over her shoulder, finally reaching her breast. When she felt him touch her there, a shock of revulsion passed through her, and without stopping to consider the consequences, she did the only thing she could think of: she spit on his hand.

The marquess stared at the spittle, a frightening light flaring in his pale eyes. "Why, you little slut," he screamed, and with a vicious jerk he tore the bodice of her dress, revealing the top of Catherine's bosom. The marquess reached for the thin camisole that was now her only covering.

Trembling with disgust, Catherine prepared herself to jerk away.

But she did not need to. Like a clap of thunder signaling a storm, a pistol shot sounded in the dis-

tance, then another. The marquess swore violently
when a door toward the back of the house slammed,
and two more shots were heard.

Spinning around, he seized Catherine, pulling her
from the bed, half-dragging, half-pushing her before him to the door, leaving one hand free to draw
out his pistol.

"My guest seems to have arrived a little earlier
than I had expected. But no matter, the end will be
the same." A shrill, ugly laugh sounded in her ear as
he forced Catherine to hobble before him down the
narrow steps of the house.

They had descended about midway when the door
at the foot of the stairs came crashing open, bringing
them to an abrupt halt. A sob of desperate joy escaped Catherine when she recognized the familiar
broad shoulders and tall figure of Adam Cameron
outlined in the doorway.

Even in the poor early-morning light, Catherine
could see the anger flame in his eyes as he took in
her torn bodice. For an instant his eyes bore into
hers, then they turned to the man behind her, their
expression now shuttered.

"Your quarrel is with me, Lynsford, not with Catherine. Release her and face me. I am the one you
want."

Catherine could feel Lynsford's breath coming in
short gasps on her neck.

His response to the duke was a high, thin laugh.
"You would like for me to release her, I am sure.
Then you and your men could make short work of
me." Another eerie, high laugh sounded, sending
chills down Catherine's spine. "But she's mine now,
Clarendon. Yes! I can see by the look in your eyes
you know what I mean. I've had her. I shall never
release her now, she is mine!"

"Why, you!" The duke started toward the stairs, a
murderous look of rage on his face.

"Hold! Or I'll shoot her!" The marquess's voice was excited, breathless with delight at the pain he had caused. "It would please me to force you to live without her, knowing it was you who caused her death. Ha! So you will back off now. The great Duke of Clarendon reduced to impotent rage, just as I have been since your father beggared mine."

Catherine shuddered as the taunting words came faster, but nothing could compare with the terror she experienced when the marquess turned the pistol he had held aimed at her head toward the duke. Dear heaven, he really intended to kill Adam! The sound of Lynsford cocking the pistol vibrated loudly in her ear, then she heard his hateful, gloating voice announce, "And now, my dear Clarendon, it is your turn to pay."

As he uttered the words, Catherine squeezed her eyes shut and with a desperate prayer launched her body upward and backward. She heard the marquess emit a startled grunt as his pistol exploded by her ear, then she felt herself lose her balance and fall toward the slight stair railing. With a loud crack it gave way, sending Catherine tumbling to the floor, barely registering the sound of another shot before she hit the floor and lost awareness.

"Miss Asterley, Miss Asterley."

Slowly the blackness around her began to recede, and Catherine distinguished a voice, an unfamiliar voice. She felt her bonds being untied and a painful rush of blood into her hands and feet. Struggling to raise her head, she looked around for the owner of the voice.

A small nondescript man with brown eyes and a pointed chin came into focus. He was looking at her anxiously, but her eyes moved to his cheek. There was no scar there.

"How?" her voice was too hoarse to use.

"His grace has been hit, but not too badly," the man answered. "Lord Lynsford only grazed his temple. All the same, he is out right now. I am Thomas Brown, miss; the duke hired me to help him with this business."

"And Lynsford?" Catherine whispered.

"Dead, miss. His grace got him before he went down himself."

A wave of fierce, uncontained joy shook Catherine. Lynsford was dead! His mad, grotesque bitterness could never threaten Adam again. Using Mr. Brown's assistance, Catherine stumbled to her feet, willing herself to walk out of the cottage despite the pain in her ankles and wrists.

Brown gave her his cloak to hide her torn bodice as he told her he had found a man living in a cottage down the road who had agreed to be their coachman to London.

"If you are up to it, miss, I shall leave you to accompany his grace while I remain here," Mr. Brown said. "There will be a magistrate to see to as well as the bodies of the deceased."

Catherine thanked him for the cloak, nodding yes to his question while her eyes were riveted to the still figure lying on the seat of the marquess's carriage. How vulnerable Adam looked, with the makeshift bandage fixed around his head. Tears spilling down her face, she gently raised his head onto her lap.

In later years she would remember little of the return trip. The knot of tension inside her unraveled the closer to London they came, and she dozed in fits and starts. The duke awoke only once; his eyes aware, he raised up to ask, "Catherine? Are you all right? And Lynsford?"

When Catherine answered that she was fine and the marquess dead, he fell back, losing consciousness immediately.

For a long time afterward Catherine stared at his

face, memorizing the strong line of his jaw, the flare
of his nostrils, the curve of his mouth. She smoothed
a lock of unruly black hair from his brow. His face at
rest looked younger; there were no lines of care or
mockery on it. She had seldom seen it so, she thought
sadly, recalling the sneer with which he had regarded
her only the night before. As soon as it was possible,
she must escape to Althea's cousin's farm, where she
would have the solitude to lick her wounds and to
try to begin her life again.

She smiled sadly. "It's a fine plan," she whispered
to the pale face in her lap, "but I am afraid it will
take me a long while to put you behind me, my fine
sir." Very carefully, lest she disturb him, Catherine
leaned over and gently placed a kiss on the duke's
brow.

27

"*O*h, my dear, you do look better." Lady de Maine's concerned eyes examined Catherine closely. It was late afternoon of the same day they had arrived at Clarendon House, and Catherine, having awakened a short while before, was standing before her open valise. It was her first opportunity to speak with Lady de Maine since the duke's aunt had embraced her tightly on her return and then sent her directly to a hot bath and bed.

"I feel a great deal better, my lady." Catherine smiled. "And his grace, what did the doctor say?"

"Dr. Fletcher says Adam's wound is only a scratch and he will be much recovered after a good rest. We've dosed him with laudanum now, but he should be awake by morning. My dear girl, there is so much to say, but first I must thank you for saving Adam. Mr. Brown has come already and told me how you sent Lynsford's shot astray. Without you, I don't know what might have happened. No, don't deny it, you are too modest, as always, child. We owe you a great, great debt."

Catherine's amber eyes were very dark as they rested on the other woman. "You owe me nothing, my lady. I cannot tell you how sorry I am to have had to hoax you. You have been so kind to me, I wish there had been a way to spare you the disappointment."

"My dear, dear girl" Lady de Maine wrapped Catherine in an embrace. "Do not fret yourself another

moment. I own I was terribly disappointed when
Adam told me. I had thought you were so well-
suited, but of course, I understand." Encircled by
Lady de Maine's warmth, Catherine surprised them
both by bursting into tears.

"Now, that's better." Lady de Maine's eyes were
glistening when Catherine at last looked up, drying
her eyes with a handkerchief. "Are you up to telling
me what happened, my dear? You don't have to if
you don't wish."

Catherine was both willing and able to tell of her
adventures, from her walk with Eustace to Brown's
appearance, only omitting the scene she had overheard in the gardens when the duke had dismissed
her in favor of Blanche Romney. To Lady de Maine
she explained that she had left Eustace because he
had begun to make insinuations whose nature she
left deliberately vague.

"Stupidly I left his protection before I should have,
and allowed the marquess to find me."

"You mustn't fault yourself, Catherine." Lady de
Maine patted her hand. "You could not have known
the madman was Lynsford. But I've some news that
may cheer you. Adam, just before he left, told me of
Anne Lynsford's *tendre* for Charles Musgrave, which
came as a complete surprise, I must say, and asked
that I get word to Charles about your abduction.
Another gallant rescue was effected when he found
Anne locked in her room and carried her away to
stay with a relative of his. They'll not have a cloud
hanging over them when they marry either, for Mr.
Brown persuaded the magistrate to describe Lynsford's cause of death as a hunting accident."

When Catherine had expressed her great pleasure
at the news, Lady de Maine cast a puzzled look at
Catherine's valise, which lay open, displaying the
meager wardrobe Catherine had possessed before
she came to London.

Seeing the glance, Catherine rallied her forces to explain quietly that she was leaving within the hour.

"But, but, you simply cannot go yet; you are not even rested and Adam will want to thank you," Lady de Maine protested, aghast.

But nothing could persuade Catherine. Adamantly she insisted she must leave to attend to affairs she had neglected.

When she saw there was nothing she could say to change Catherine's mind, Lady de Maine left to see to a carriage, muttering about the idiocy of some people not quite under her breath.

With a sad little smile, for she had heard her, Catherine set about her last task, a note to the duke. She was, she wrote, pleased to have been of service to him, and though urgent business forced her abrupt departure, she hoped he would believe she was most sincere when she wished him a speedy recovery. She ended by asking him to send her wages to Althea in Bath and made no mention at all of her own future address. Then, after a great deal of thought, she signed the brief letter simply "Catherine."

"Oh, miss!" It was Peg, her eyes round as saucers, looking from Catherine to the valise and back again. Taking a deep breath and even essaying a smile, Catherine turned to make her last good-bye. It was not easy bidding the faithful little maid farewell, particularly when Peg's brown eyes filled with tears, but at last it was done and Catherine was walking down the long hallway, her valise, which she would not allow Peg to carry for her, in her hand.

To reach the stairs she had to pass the duke's room, and though common sense urged her not to, she turned the handle. Relief flooded through her when she saw how much better he looked. His face was not so drawn or so pale, and he looked both vulnerable and excessively handsome all at the same time. It was a potent combination.

Catherine longed with such an intensity to stay by his bed that she was frightened. It was imperative that she be gone before he could awaken. He held such a power over her, she was not at all sure she would be able to leave him if he asked her again to be his mistress. Not that he would, of course, he was far too disgusted with her, but Catherine did not think she wanted to test the point.

Downstairs Lady de Maine was waiting for her, the sympathetic gleam in her eyes revealing that she knew more about the origin of the tears brimming in Catherine's eyes than Catherine might have wished. Lady de Maine with exquisite tact said nothing, however, only telling Catherine that the coach was at her disposal and forcing Catherine to take a substantial purse as an advance on her salary. "You will need to eat, after all," she declared, closing Catherine's hand over it. Afraid she would embarrass herself by breaking into sobs, Catherine kissed the wrinkled cheek offered to her and fled out the door.

At her request the coachman conveyed her to a posting inn on the edge of the city, where she obtained a seat to Winchester. When she arrived there, she found a modest but comfortable inn and immediately sent Althea her address, cautioning her not to confide it to anyone. Catherine did not think the duke would pursue her of his own accord, but she remembered her sighting of Rudolph. She was not taking the chance that Rudolph might somehow learn of her connection with Clarendon and convince the duke that it was his duty to assist in tracking the runaway ward who had recently been his employee.

Convinced she had eluded pursuit, Catherine was outwardly serene as she waited for Allie. Only her dreams betrayed how little the new life upon which she was poised concerned her and how wrenchingly her stay in London had affected her.

28

"And you let her go—just like that, without a
by-your-leave, with no word of thanks or farewell?" The Duke of Clarendon regarded his aunt
with angry astonishment.

Lady de Maine did not seem in the least put out
with his temper and returned his angry stare plac-
idly. "Well, Adam, I did give her an advance," she
explained reasonably. "One hundred pounds is hardly
nothing, and I did wish her farewell." Lady de Maine
watched with a slight smile as her nephew resumed
the pacing he had begun the instant she had informed him of Catherine's departure.

When the duke had awakened late that morning,
Dr. Fletcher had pronounced him fit to rise but unfit
to leave the house. The bandage had even been
removed, all bleeding having stopped, and a long
thin gash was painly visible.

The condition of his wound was of little interest to
the duke, however. When upon awakening he had
asked for Catherine, Lady de Maine had perforce to
tell him she had left the house the day before
without a word as to her destination. The unexpected news had sent him into a towering rage, which
had sustained him through rising, dressing, and a
cup of coffee. After that poor excuse for a breakfast,
he had "ordered"—there was no other word for it—
his aunt to accompany him to the library to explain
the unacceptable state of affairs.

"But where could she have gone, just like that?" Adam asked, as much to himself as to his aunt.

"I am sure I do not know," she replied, intent on smoothing a wrinkle from her dress. "Catherine would tell no one her destination. Do you know nothing of her at all, Adam? Doe she have any relatives, perhaps?"

"No, I do not know. Only Althea Reed in Bath." The duke's voice sounded distinctly snappish, which Lady de Maine thought might or might not have been ascribed to his aching head. "And you say you could not have contrived to delay her departure until I had a chance to speak with her? It was only the matter of a night."

"I did try, Adam," Lady de Maine replied, once again taking no offense at his sharp tone. "She was quite determined to go immediately, and you know Catherine when she has her mind quite made up. I suppose I too find it curious she should wish to leave so abruptly." There was a question lingering in the eyes Lady de Maine raised to her nephew. "Almost as curious as the manner in which she left Eustace that night at the gardens. She never did adequately explain why she rushed off without any escort."

Lady de Maine's question was rewarded with no answer, only an abrupt movement that presented to her the duke's broad back as he stared with a brooding frown out the window at the garden beyond.

A knock at the door interrupted them. In answer to the duke's summons, Davies entered, dismay apparent on his long face.

"Your grace, a man ..." Davies' wounded tones paused over the word to emphasize just how far from a gentleman he considered the caller to be. "A man is at the door, demanding to see you. Despite my best efforts to deny him access, he insists he must see you on serious business regarding a Catherine Spenser. I have assured him there is no one here with that name, but he is most insistent."

The duke's manner changed subtly at Davies' news. There was a new, keen, intent light in his gray eyes, but he hid his interest well, only drawling in lazy tones, "Send him in, Davies. It will be quite all right. And, ah, thank you for your efforts."

With a stiff nod the still-perturbed Davies accepted his employer's commendation and left to summon their mystery caller.

"Catherine Spenser?" Lady de Maine asked, her eyes wide with question. "Do you believe she is our Catherine?"

"We shall see," replied her nephew, his eyes taking on their hooded look.

Within a few moments Davies returned to announce Baron Rudolph Spenser, before he left, closing the door behind him.

Catherine might well have laughed in surprise had she been able to see the Rudolph Spenser, who several minutes later was still standing before the imposing closed doors of the duke's library. Gone was the menacing man who had threatened her; in his place was a man of hesitant manner who shifted nervously from one foot to the other.

It had not taken Rudolph long to decide his ward was Clarendon's mistress; companions or governesses were not dressed as fashionably as she had been. Filled with the courage his legal status as guardian gave him, and secure in the assumption that dukes were elderly, frail men, he had decided it was his right to demand a payment for the duke's continued use of her or, if that failed, her return. Rudolph, his eyes gleaming over the enormous wealth displayed so elegantly around him, had entered the duke's study mentally recalculating the sum he could command, only to be stopped dead by reality. The man behind the desk was not the least old or frail, but in the prime of his life, with broad shoulders, muscled arms, and strange, hooded silver eyes, which at this moment were regarding him as if he might be dinner.

"Ahem, your grace," he protested, smiling obsequiously and rolling his eyes in Lady de Maine's direction.

"This is my aunt, Lady de Maine. State your business, sir." The duke's voice was curt and commanded Rudolph's immediate respect.

"Yes, your grace. It's just, er, that my business is, er, well just between men."

"I have nothing to hide, Baron. Lady de Maine is very like my mother."

Rudolph flushed, aware he had been left to stand like a supplicant before a powerful lord. Bucking up the remnants of his courage, he reminded himself that Catherine was his ward.

"I am Catherine Spenser's guardian," he informed the duke. He waited, but there was no sign of recognition on the dark, imposing face regarding him implacably.

"I don't know a Catherine Spenser," the duke said at last, idly waving a gleaming letter-opener.

"But, but I saw her in your carriage," Rudolph stuttered, his eyes darting to the thin, dangerous object in the duke's hand. "It was last Friday in Bond Street."

"Let me see if I can get this straight," the duke drawled softly, the blade of the letter-opener pointed directly at the baron. "You are looking for a ward whom you have misplaced. Is that correct, Baron?"

Rudolph could feel the sweat trickle down his neck. "Yes . . . No! That is, no, she ran away," he cried. "She is headstrong, always has been, with no one but that wastrel father to look after her, and him gone most of the time. Letty and I found her a perfectly good husband, perhaps a bit older than Catherine, it's true, but well-to-do, who could have given her everything she wanted. But did she appreciate our efforts? No, indeed. The first thing we knew, she was gone."

"And what did you think to ask of me, Baron?" The silky sound of the duke's voice should have been a warning to Rudolph, but the next words were too much what he wanted to hear for him to exercise good judgment. "Would a pouch of gold ease the pain of your ward's disappearance, perhaps?"

Rudolph's eyes lit up. "Yes, your grace. She owes us something. It was her father, the old baron, who impoverished us . . ." Rudolph's voice trailed off, the duke had uncoiled to his full height.

"Willing to sell your own family, Baron?" he asked softly, sending the blood rushing into Rudolph's face. "A rather shabby guardian, I'd say, wouldn't you, Aunt Em?"

"Indeed I do," that lady agreed fiercely, her eyes snapping at the beleaguered baron.

"Well, Baron, I do not know where Catherine Spenser is. However, I intend to find her, and when I do . . ."

As a pregnant silence filled the room, Rudolph's frightened eyes were drawn back to his tormentor. Satisfied that he had Rudolph's attention, the duke continued, "When I do find Miss Spenser, Baron, I intend to make her my wife."

Rudolph's mouth fell open, and his throat worked to produce a strangled sound.

"And I will brook no interference from the likes of you, Baron," the duke continued, leaning forward menacingly, "now, or after I find her. If I hear you have approached her ever again, for any reason, I shall personally see that you are ruined. Do you comprehend, Baron?"

Rudolph, looking at those hard eyes, had no doubt whatsoever that the man before him could and would ruin him if he chose to do so. Nodding rapidly,

Rudolph managed to force, "Yes, your grace," through stiff lips.

"That will be all, then, Baron. You may go."

Without another word Rudolph scuttled out of the room, profoundly thankful to have escaped so lightly. He had been certain the duke was going to challenge him to a duel, an action that would have been tantamount to a death sentence. He would use his reprieve to get himself to Northumberland as quickly as possible and put all thoughts of Catherine and the Duke of Clarendon from his mind.

"Damn!" The word exploded from the duke as he banged the desk with his fist. A surge of memories passed through his mind: Catherine flawlessly passing muster that first night at dinner; Catherine charming the *ton* with her pretty manners; Catherine proudly flinging his invitation to become his mistress in his face.

How could he have missed the truth? Perhaps he had not wanted to know. As long as she was only an actress in a provincial theater company, he could pretend all he felt was lust. One did not fall in love with actresses.

On the desperate ride to Lynsford's hunting box, he had begun to face his feelings. Glad as he was to avenge Gerald, the desperation was all for Catherine. He had determined that he would never let her go, no matter how much she resisted, though even then it was not marriage he had in mind. It had taken her miserable guardian to show him what he really wanted.

"Damn!" he swore again, though softly this time.

Lady de Maine sat watching the play of emotions on her nephew's face with a small smile. Perhaps, she thought, all was not yet lost. Clearing her throat, she gained his attention. "I think I shall give it out that Catherine is still quite ill, until you decide what you want to do, my dear."

"I am afraid, Aunt Emily"—a rueful smile lit his eyes—"that the question is not what the Duke of Clarendon wants to do, but what the runaway ward of a down-at-the-heels baron wishes."

"Ah," Lady de Maine said, studying her fingertips for a moment, then continuing as if she had made a decision. "Adam, I was not sure you were not gammoning the baron when you said you intended to marry Catherine. But if you were serious, I think you can have some hope as to your prospects. I may not have known Catherine's identity, but there is one thing about her of which I am sure: she is very much in love with you, whether you deserve it or not. If you do want her, you will have to find her and tell her so. Put properly, I daresay she'll come around."

"I shall just have to try, won't I?" said her nephew, a very determined light gleaming in his eyes.

29

*C*atherine reached down to free her skirt from a jutting piece of stone. With an ease bespeaking practice she then jumped lightly to the ground, one hand extended for balance. With nothing to do but wait for Althea's arrival, Catherine had taken a great many walks in the neighborhood of the inn. The landlord had kindly pointed out this field, which slanted upward to a far corner, the highest point of land around. There, under a leafy apple tree, she would sketch or simply gaze at the neat countryside around her, resolutely not thinking of London, her friends there, and most especially not thinking of Adam Cameron. He was gone from her life and that was that, or so she told herself over and over.

Fleecy white clouds dotted a clear, intensely blue sky, and Catherine took off her bonnet, not caring that she would add to the freckles on her nose. She was no longer the elegant Miss Asterley. Her heavy hair was unconfined, for without Peg's assistance it was too difficult to manage into a fashionable hairstyle, and her light muslin skirt was plain enough to allow her to sit upon the ground without compunction.

A movement by the lower stone wall caught her eye. She could see a man was climbing over it, and she noted with envy how his close-fitting breeches did not catch on it. The man started up the hill, and even from that distance Catherine could see he was a large man, wide-shouldered with a narrow waist. His

hair she could see now was like . . . Her heart skipped
a beat, then began to hammer painfully in her chest.
There were not many men so tall with hair the color
of ebony. A frightful panic overwhelmed her. Frantically she looked around as if a hiding place might
miraculously appear. None did, and she rose slowly
to face the approaching figure.

The Duke of Clarendon felt, Catherine would have
been surprised to learn, as anxious as she. Despite
what his aunt had told him, he was not at all certain
of Catherine's feelings. Gad, he had almost forgotten
how lovely she was. Her fiery dark hair, gleaming in
the sun, cascaded down her back like a silky water-
fall. He could see her wide amber eyes now, and her
soft full lips. Even her nose, with its sprinkling of
freckles, looked adorable to him. Her rose-petal-soft
skin was flushed, he noticed, pleased by this evidence that he could still affect her.

He stopped a few feet from her, and when their
eyes met, Catherine nearly gasped aloud at the force
with which their wills seemed to clash. After an eternity during which neither spoke, the duke, his brow
raised fractionally, broke the silence.

"I must say, Miss Spenser, you certainly have given
me the devil of a time finding you," he said in
greeting, if greeting it was.

Catherine stood staring into the dark handsome
face above her, searching for an explanation of his
sudden appearance. His face revealed little, though
she could detect a new line or two around his eyes.
Suddenly her eyes opened wide.

"Oh!" was all she could say as it came to her that
the duke knew her true name.

Ignoring that exclamation of distress completely,
the duke continued to address his own concerns. "I
wonder if you will be so good as to explain why you
left London without a word?"

"I did not leave without a word," Catherine retorted, incensed by his unbearably cool manner. She had not seen him in two weeks, and he did not even think to say hello, how are you, before chastising her as if she were still his employee.

"I bade Lady de Maine farewell. You were asleep, and I could hardly awaken you. I took care to leave you a note. Besides, you had no more business with me. But tell me—"

"No more business with you!" The duke's dark brow drew into a furious scowl. "What can you mean? You saved my life. I might at the very least have been afforded the opportunity to express my thanks."

Catherine's eyes fell away from his angry scowl to inspect the tip of her slipper. Her head still bent, she shrugged. "There was no need for thanks; anyone would have done the same. Besides"—Catherine raised her head, her expressive eyes plainly revealing remorse—"it was my fault you were placed in such danger in the first place. I stupidly put myself in Lynsford's hands."

"Ah, I am curious about that." The duke folded his arms before him, his eyes narrowed upon Catherine.

The color came and went in Catherine's cheeks, and she made a vague gesture.

"Well, I left Eustace when he . . . Oh, really, the matter is over and done with now. I want to know—"

"No, Catherine." The duke's voice had grown quiet. "The matter is far from over. Shall I tell you why I think you left Eustace?"

Catherine neither moved nor spoke, unable to break her eyes away from the hold the duke's gaze held over her.

"I think you ran from Eustace because you overheard a conversation between Blanche and myself, and you realized that Eustace was a party to arranging that conversation. You were so infuriated by his conniving that you immediately left his company. Isn't that correct?"

Catherine dragged her eyes from his, remembering the conversation she had heard, hearing again the words that had hurt her so deeply. Determined the arrogant man before here would not know the damage he had inflicted upon her, she responded with a crisp nod of her head. "That is exactly what occurred. You are a wizard, your grace. I simply could not bear that fat toad's presence a moment longer and ran away headlong into trouble. Happily it all turned out right in the end, and there was no harm done. But I am curious—"

"But it has not turned out right in the end, at all, in my opinion. How can it be right when you have hidden yourself away here?"

"I am not hidden away," Catherine protested with an appalling disregard for the truth. "I had always meant to come here. Althea and I planned it before I left Bath."

"You left no address where I or Aunt Emily might write you, and you instructed Miss Reed not to divulge your whereabouts to me," the duke corrected her remorselessly.

"I had my reasons," Catherine snapped, feeling as if she had been most unfairly put on the defensive.

"I wonder if your reasons have anything to do with a certain Rudolph Spenser?" The duke's voice was silky.

At the outright mention of Rudolph, Catherine gasped.

"Ah, I see that the mere mention of the baron's name alarms you. Therefore, I must assume your precipitous flight and subsequent disappearance have at least something to do with a desire to avoid him. That you made it difficult for me to find you, as well, can only mean that you thought that I might turn you over to the good baron."

Long thick lashes swiftly covered Catherine's eyes.

Put so baldly in that drawling, slightly derisive voice, the thought made her feel shabby.

"As you must know, the baron is my guardian, your grace," she defended herself softly. "The law stands on his side. I did not think you would have a choice."

"I see," was the icy, unmollified reply. "You thought that Miss Reed would have a choice, but that I would not."

Catherine flinched as the duke's voice flicked her contemptuously, but she straightened her shoulders and bravely looked into the duke's glinting eyes. "If you will recall, things between us were not exactly smooth then. I cannot be blamed for thinking you might not wish to risk a scandal by defying my legal guardian. But I am sorry you had to become involved with him. I hope the interview with him was not too dreadful."

"Don't distress yourself over Rudolph." The duke's voice sounded oddly gruff. "I needed something to squash that day and he provided a perfect target. I was indebted to him for his timely appearance. Besides, he, at least, was honest about who you are, Miss Spenser, daughter of a baron."

The accusation stung. She had deceived him, and although she had had good reasons for doing so, she could not feel glad about it. Still, when he had hired her, she had been an actress, just as he had thought. She had not deceived him about that. How odious of him to come all this way merely to sit in judgment of her!

Her eyes flashed at the thought. "You wanted an actress, your grace, and I was an actress. You would not have hired me if you had known I was also a baron's daughter."

"You might have told me later, when you were entrenched as Miss Asterley."

The reasonable-sounding suggestion goaded Catherine's ready temper. "Ha!" she scoffed at the absurdity of the idea. "If I had told you later, you would not have believed me, you never believed me about anything; or, if you had chosen to believe me, you would doubtless have accused me of trying to obligate you to marry me. You might even have thought you had to marry me."

"And would marriage to me have been so awful?" Though the question was asked softly, the sound of it echoed like a shout in the silence that followed.

The duke had reached, at last, the heart of his concern, but years of concealing his feelings prevented him from letting Catherine know how important her answer was to him. He waited tensely for it, but Catherine, searching his face, could see only a bland, indifferent expression as he asked if her dearest wish in the world would be "so awful." It was too much. Her control snapped, and before she could prevent herself, she cried out at him for being so cruel to her.

"Quit this," she demanded, aware that betraying tears were welling in her eyes. "What game are you playing with me now? Do you know so little of me that you think I would want to wed a man who does not want me? You have made it plain enough that you do not care for me and that you love another!"

With a little sob, Catherine whirled about, trying desperately to hide the tears coursing down her cheeks. The duke had heard what he wanted to hear, and for a moment he merely stood looking at the proud stance of the young woman turned away from him.

"Catherine," he said at last, reaching for her. "No, don't go away. I've been such a fool, please let me explain. Ah, that got your attention, I see. It's not often I humble myself."

The duke was holding her by the shoulders, and

though her vision was blurred by tears, Catherine could not mistake the tender warmth in his eyes.

"I am so very sorry you were hurt by that scene at Vauxhall," he began, kissing away the tears in her eyes. "Blanche Romney has not mattered to me since she came to my bed the night her engagement to Romney was announced. I realized then how very little there was behind her inviting exterior. I have taken advantage of what she offered often enough, but with no real feeling for Blanche. I was using her that night to goad you to jealousy. Not that I knew you would overhear us. I knew nothing of their plan, but I did intend to return Blanche to the party looking well-used. I hoped the sight would hurt you enough to pierce your resistance to me. Instead, I nearly lost you to Lynsford's madness. Catherine, can you ever forgive me for what he did to you?"

Catherine had to force herself to look serious. She wanted to shout with joy, for at last she knew her love loved her, but first she must wipe that haunted look from his face.

"There is nothing to forgive." Her amber eyes looked steadily into his. "Lynsford did tear my dress and would have done much more, but you arrived before he had the opportunity. He said he had had me only to taunt you."

Catherine had thought her words would lighten the duke's expression, but he continued to frown. "And can you forgive me for all the hurtful things I have said to you?"

Words deserted her, then. She was too aware of his face close to hers, of the familiar clean scent of him, and of his arms holding her. She could only nod mutely.

"Then you'll marry me!" He grinned triumphantly.

A wild sweet joy coursed through her as his mouth captured hers, and she responded ardently. When they drew apart quite some time later, the duke's

eyes were a smoky gray as he regarded the beauty in
his arms. Her mouth trembling from his kisses, Catherine returned his look, not shrinking from the raw
desire in his eyes. It was no secret that she wanted
him. With one finger she reached out to trace the
strong mouth so close above her, an impish smile
forming on her lips.

"Is there any need for me to say, yes, Adam, I
shall marry you, or was that a command?"

"Minx," Adam whispered in her ear, drawing her
to him again. "Perhaps, you need more persuading?"
When he had thoroughly explored her soft lips, he
kissed her eyes, her cheeks, the hollow of her neck,
and then, once again, her lips.

"Now, tell me you will marry me, my love, and
never, ever leave my side," he commanded softly.

A dazzling smile dawned on Catherine's lovely face.
"I will marry you, Adam Cameron, and I will never,
ever leave your side," she repeated.

For a long, long moment they regarded each other
steadily, then, in a husky whisper that ignited a flame
in his silver eyes, she added, "You have made me so
very happy, my love. Come, kiss me again."

About the Author

Emma Lange is a graduate of the University of California at Berkeley, where she studied European history. She and her husband live in the midwest and pursue, as they are able, interests in traveling and in sailing.

AMOROUS ESCAPADES

☐	THE UNRULY BRIDE by Vanessa Gray.	(134060—$2.50)
☐	THE DUKE'S MESSENGER by Vanessa Gray.	(138856—$2.50)
☐	THE DUTIFUL DAUGHTER by Vanessa Gray.	(142179—$2.50)
☐	THE RECKLESS GAMBLER by Vanessa Gray.	(137647—$2.50)
☐	THE ABANDONED BRIDE by Edith Layton.	(135652—$2.50)
☐	THE DISDAINFUL MARQUIS by Edith Layton.	(145879—$2.50)
☐	FALSE ANGEL by Edith Layton.	(138562—$2.50)
☐	THE INDIAN MAIDEN by Edith Layton.	(143019—$2.50)
☐	RED JACK'S DAUGHTER by Edith Layton.	(144880—$2.50)
☐	LADY OF SPIRIT by Edith Layton.	(145178—$2.50)
☐	THE NOBLE IMPOSTER by Mollie Ashton.	(129156—$2.25)
☐	LORD CALIBAN by Ellen Fitzgerald.	(134761—$2.50)
☐	A NOVEL ALLIANCE by Ellen Fitzgerald.	(132742—$2.50)
☐	THE IRISH HEIRESS by Ellen Fitzgerald.	(136594—$2.50)
☐	ROGUE'S BRIDE by Ellen Fitzgerald.	(140435—$2.50)

Prices slightly higher in Canada.